DAMON & PETE:
Playing with Fire

K.C. WELLS
writing as TANTALUS

For Hannah
♥ K C
Wells

Copyright information
This is a work of fiction. Names, characters, places, and incidents either are the product of the author's imagination or are used fictitiously, and any resemblance to actual persons, living or dead, business establishments, events, or locales is entirely coincidental.

Damon & Pete: Playing with Fire
Copyright © 2019 by K.C. Wells writing as Tantalus

Cover Art by Meredith Russell
Photography by: KJ Heath Photography

The trademarked products mentioned in this book are the property of their respective owners, and are recognized as such.

All Rights Reserved. No part of this book may be reproduced or transmitted in any form or by any means, including electronic or mechanical, including photocopying, recording, or by any information storage and retrieval system without the written permission of the Publisher, except where permitted by law.

This volume comprises the five short stories of the series, Damon & Pete: Playing with Fire:

Summer Heat
After
Consequences
Limits
Fractures

It also contains the short Valentine's Day story, Pete's Treat.

Many thanks to those who helped me with this series:
Wulf Francú Godgluck, a great editor and inspiration.
Jack Parton and Alexander Cheves, for their expertise.

And of course, my wonderful beta team who read everything so carefully –
Jason, Daniel, Helena, Debra, Sharon and Mardee.

SUMMER HEAT

TANTALUS

SUMMER HEAT

Pete and his hunky bear of a neighbor, Damon, are always competing about something. So when Damon makes a bet on the outcome of their next poker game, Pete is up for it, even if the terms are a little…unusual.
If Damon wins, he gets to do Whatever. He. Wants. Only thing is, Pete has no idea that Damon has a dark side…

Summer Heat

"Are you ready for me, baby?" His fingers traced the contours of my abs, pulling a shiver from me.

How long have I waited to hear him say those words? And so much more besides…

"Yes." The word came out as a croak, and I cursed my tightened throat.

His breath was hot on the back of my neck. He chuckled, a rich sound that made all the hairs on my arms stand on end. "You don't sound too sure." I caught my breath as he slid his hand lower, until he was there, poised right above my aching cock.

Yeah, there. Wrap your hand around it.

"I'm s-sure," I stammered, willing him to move.

Seconds past. More seconds. And still that hand was firm against my lower belly.

Oh, come on, Damon, please….

His fingers stroked the base and my breathing hitched. *Fuck, yeah.* I waited for more, eyes closed, ready to scream when he started heading north.

Touch me, damn you. TOUCH ME.

"Your skin is warm." Soft lips brushed over my shoulder and I shuddered to feel his hot tongue lick a line down my back. I pulled against the restraints around my wrists, silently urging him to go lower, that agile tongue almost reaching the cleft of my ass. Damon, the fucker, had to show me who was in control, however. I gritted my teeth when that mouth began working its way up my spine instead. I couldn't stop shuddering when he sank his teeth into the nape of my neck.

"I-it's a hot night." Fuck, could I not manage one goddamn sentence without my voice quavering?

His voice rumbled next to my ear, deep and dark. "And it's gonna get hotter."

I gasped when he took my ear lobe between his teeth and tugged hard, sending a shockwave of pain through me.

"That got your attention."

Like I could ignore the feel of his body, wider than mine and thick with muscle. The coarse hair on his chest brushed against my back, and there it was, fucking *finally*, his cock, hard and hot, rubbing against my ass, dripping pre-cum on me. I pushed back eagerly, wanting more, my own dick stiff and poking upward.

Damon laughed, the type of laugh that got me all kinds of hot and bothered, yet still managed to turn my spinal fluid to ice at the same time. "I'm beginning to think you lost our bet on purpose." He rocked his hips, sliding his solid thick meat through my crack. His hot breath caressed my ear. "This what you were thinking about while we were playing poker, Pete? You imagining my cock rubbing over your little boy hole?" His growl reverberated through me when he pressed himself against my back. "Is that why your playing was for shit tonight? Your mind was already contemplating me fucking ya?"

"No," I protested. I'd played to win—hadn't I? Even if it had sounded like a joke when Damon first suggested it. We were always so damn competitive: which of us had the best yard, the most Christmas lights—you name it, we'd try to outdo each other on it. But then Damon had taken me aside after the last poker game with the boys, after he'd lost a packet, and had wanted to bet on the outcome of the next game. Some incentive, he said, to make the game a little more... interesting.

If I won, Damon got to clean my car for six months. His next suggestion made my throat seize up, just as easily as if his beefy paw had clamped around it.

If I lost, he could do whatever he wanted with me.

He was right, of course. I'd had the worse luck that night, and it was no surprise to me at the end of the evening that I'd lost, big time.

Except this didn't feel like I'd lost. Not when I found myself naked and shackled to a fucking St. Andrew's Cross in Damon's goddamn basement.

Who was I kidding? I'd played to lose, all right.

"Oh, so I got this all wrong?" Damon stepped back, and my body was already at war with myself for the loss of his intimate, damp, warm body. "You don't want me to fuck you?"

I froze, and then shivered in my restraints. *God, yes, I want to feel you fuck me.*

"Bastard," I ground out under my breath. I pulled at the shackles around my wrists.

"If you got something to say, Petey-boy—"

His fingers grasped my hair, lips brushing over my ear as his hot words spilled out like liquid heat. "—just come out an' say it." He pulled away from me abruptly, leaving me cold, almost at bursting point with longing and need.

For fuck's sake, just say it. It wasn't like I hadn't been lusting after Damon for months, ever since he'd moved into the house next door. I swear, every time I looked out of my window, there he was on his front lawn, shirtless. *Why the fuck does he always have to be bare chested?* All that hot, silky fur, glistening in the summer heat, that dense chest with its firm, muscled pecs... Okay, he was no Mr. Olympia. Damon had the slightest hint of a belly but *God*, you could *smell* the power in his large frame, just watching the sweat breaking out and glistening on his big shoulders and thick arms. I'd spent months watching him from afar, drooling over his Latino body, fantasizing.... And here I was, at his mercy, knowing *exactly* what I wanted to happen.

"I... I want you to fuck me," I said, trying to keep my voice from shaking.

Damon stepped closer, his fingers ghosting over my right butt cheek. "I didn't catch that."

Oh, you fucking bastard.

"Fuck me. I need you to fuck me." Christ, I sounded like I was begging, and in that moment, I couldn't have cared less.

He stepped up close and took both cheeks in his large hands. I could feel the calluses on his fingers biting into my soft flesh when he squeezed hard. "This white boy ass of yours is too fucking pale. I'm not sliding my dick into you until these cheeks are burning pink, and as hot as your tight little hole."

Shitshitshitshitshit....

He pressed up against me, forcing the breath from me as my body was flattened against the smooth wood of the cross. "But who's to say you're tight? I've seen you at that bar downtown." He bit into my shoulder and I cried out. "Yeah, you're a regular little slut, ain't ya, Petey-boy? You love taking it up the ass." His cock, hard as fuck, pushed at my crack again, only more insistently now. "Yeah, you can't wait for it."

"You... you saw me?" *Fuck.*

Damon snorted. "Why'd you think I made that bet? I've been dyin' to tap this boy booty for months."

I bit back a grunt when he pushed a spit-slick finger roughly into my hole. *Christ, if that's his finger...*

"Oh yeah," he purred. "Nice 'n' tight. You like that?" He slid it deeper, making my whole body shiver. "Someone's boy pussy is a greedy little fuck." His finger twisted inside me, seeking...

Oh God, no...

"By the time I'm through with you..." He slid his finger out, brought it to my lips and shoved it into my mouth, where I had no choice but to suck it. "You're not gonna be able to use this hole for a week."

I couldn't help myself. I pushed back, clenching my ass and trapped that thick cock between my cheeks. Damon shuddered, shaking against me.

He pulled back. "Not yet, baby, remember?" A large hand stroked over my ass and squeezed one cheek.

He's not... he's not really gonna spank me... is he?

God, the relief that flowed through me when nothing happened. I breathed easier, letting the restraints take my weight as his hand left my ass.

Then those fingers were back, sliding over my abs, only this time there was no gentle exploration of my skin. *This* time Damon grabbed hold of my tits and *squeezed,* before pinching my nipples once more. Pinching, twisting, until I was pleading with him to stop. "D-Damon, that fucking *hurts.*"

Damon's breathed teased my ear. "Oh, sensitive little titties. That's good to know." He nuzzled into my neck while he carried on tormenting my nipples, making me wince. "Should get them pierced, baby," he cooed, his voice deep and seductive.

"Damon, *please.*"

He ignored me, rolling his hips and grinding his erect cock against my ass while he tugged and twisted the now tender nubs. His teeth grazed my neck, biting gently and then sucking at the skin. I let my head fall back against his shoulder, eyes closed, letting the sensations build. My mind was really struggling to fight against the onslaught. My body? Was fucking *Judas*.

"Yeah, I'm thinkin' these would look real cute with little hoops through 'em. Something to tug on." He laughed and the sound reverberated throughout the basement. "You like that idea, Pete? Me piercing your tight little nipples?" His fingers pinched the taut flesh.

I wanted the ache to stop. And yet the more it continued, the harder my dick got.

Damon & Pete: Playing with Fire

Damon released my nipples and I sagged against him. He pushed me roughly against the cross, and that hand caressed my ass, those cursed fingers trickling over my skin like molten liquid, trailing up the curve of my spine. "Arch your back. Stick that ass out for me." I complied, my legs shaking. Then his hand was gone. "Ready?"

I wanted to yell, *NO*, but the word came out as a strangled cry when that first stinging slap landed on my ass cheek. "Fuck!"

Damon growled. "That? That was just the start, Petey-boy."

"I *hate* it when you call me tha—*fuuuuck*!" Another slap, this time on the other cheek, but harder. "Shit, that hurts!" My butt felt hot, I could still feel the sting. This was *not* fun. This was *not* what I was here for.

"Shut up and take it, boy." The flat of his hand met my left cheek, the pain exploding into an intense fire. A harsh cry had barely left my lips when he did it again to the other cheek.

"Not your fucking *boy*, Damon," I growled out through gritted teeth. I yelped when he grabbed my ass hard and squeezed the fiery flesh. His teeth met my shoulder again, sending ripples of pain down my spine, and I screamed.

"When you're in *my* playroom, tied up and ready for *my* cock, that makes you *my* boy for the night. You got that?" he grunted as he continued with his spanking, building up speed. Only now the slaps were landing harder, faster, the pain growing, spreading like wild fire over my skin. I whimpered with each blow, disgusted with myself when the whimpers became sobs. My ass was on fire, the flesh scorching. I tried to edge out of his reach, but there was nowhere to go. Blow after blow landed on the fleshiest part of my ass, less time elapsing between each one until it was almost constant.

It took a moment or two for me to realize that something had changed.

Damon didn't let up, there was no change there. He alternated between cheeks, grunting with each hard slap of his wide hand across my heated ass. But the sharpness of the blows seemed to... fade, to morph, tingles shooting up my spine, playing along my taint and making my thighs shake. My knees were numb, but *fuck*, my balls drew up tight. I was losing myself to the intimacy of his hand, the strength and pressure of each blow, skating along that delicate line between pain and pleasure, letting them consume me. My lips trembled, ready to ask the words that *begged* to drip off my tongue... *thank you, more, please, can I have more?*

"Yeah, that's it," Damon purred. "Feels good, doesn't it?"

It felt like there was a direct link to my cock. So much so that I sniveled when he stopped. God, the relief, though, as the pain ebbed away.

Relief that was short-lived when Damon grabbed my ass—*hard*—causing me to yelp once more. His fingers gripped the sore flesh and I bit back the scream that was right there in my throat. Relief once more when he released me. When nothing happened for a moment, I tensed, trying to anticipate his next move. My head was in turmoil.

But I wasn't about to back out. Not now. Red hot shame coursed through me at the thought that in spite of the discomfort, verging on pain, I still wanted more.

There was movement behind me and the

breath stuttered in my throat when Damon spread my cheeks and I felt that first swipe of his tongue over my ring.

"Oh Jesus, *yes*." I pushed back, wanting more, and growled when he stopped. That fucking *tease*.

Damon reached around and pinched my sore nipples. I winced, but he twisted them between his thumbs and forefingers while he moved slowly up my body. I could feel the rasp of his hair as he pressed against me with his full weight. He thundered in my ear. "I'm in charge here, Pete. And we'll get to the part where I eat your ass, but when *I* decide." His lips were on my neck. Rough fingers stroked through my hair and grabbed hold. I gasped when my head was jerked back and a hot mouth took mine in a bruising kiss, teeth clicking. He released me and his mouth was on my neck, only this time he was biting the skin, sucking at it until I knew there'd be a mark when he was done.

My heart pounded at the thought. Damon's mark, where anyone could see it. Christ, that was fucking sexy.

Damon licked and sucked his way down my back, his nails raking the skin, making me tense up. When he reached my ass, he laid a wet kiss on my right cheek, before sinking his teeth into the flesh and biting me.

"Fucking *hell*, Damon," I choked out. The man was far too fond of using his teeth.

That menacing laugh echoed through my soul. "Can't help myself, Petey-boy. I see this plump ass right in front me, just *cryin' out* for me to mark it." He grabbed a handful of ass and did it again, only this time he slid a finger over my hole. I shuddered, my whole body spasming at his touch and the fucker *laughed*, the bastard. He rubbed over my balls and along the length of my steel dick. I closed my eyes, only one thing on my mind—Damon's mouth on my cock.

But by now, I knew better than to ask. When he squeezed my balls, pulling down on them, stretching the skin taut, I wanted to scream.

"You got a pretty little dick, Pete," Damon murmured appreciatively. "Nice sac, too. Feel heavy, full of cum. Only, you don't get to."

"What?" I stiffened, not sure I'd heard him right.

"You don't get to cum." I could hear the smile in his voice.

Oh, you have got to be fucking kidding me.

"Damon, fuck, man, I'm close as it is." I glanced down to where a shiny thread of pre-cum oozed from my slit. Watching his hand reach around to stroke my shaft was fucking *hot*. I groaned as he brushed his palm over the head, smearing the sticky fluid along the length of my dick, and then tucked his thumbnail right into my slit.

Fucking hell.

"Then you're gonna have to work hard, Petey-boy. 'Cause if you cum, I'll have to punish ya."

"Punish?" Just the word sent shivers coursing through me. The prospect should've had me reacting with anger or fear. Why, then, was my heart beating so fast? My breathing so rapid?

Damon's barbarous laugh rebounded. "Yeah, I got your number, Pete. When I first laid eyes on ya, I said to myself, 'now that boy is pure vanilla.' But you're not, are ya? I can feel it from here." His fingers dug into the soft flesh of my ass as he spread me wide. A slow tongue licked from my tailbone down to my balls, and I shuddered. He blew warm air over my hole, making me clench tight. Damon's chuckle vibrated through my crease. "Like that's gonna keep me out. C'mon, Pete. Show me your pretty little hole. Let me in. I really wanna have my full of it before I fuck ya."

Fuck. That hot tide of shame flushed through me at his words. Sex had *never* been like this. I pushed out with my muscles, feeling my hole loosen.

"Good boy," he grunted, running his finger over my ring. "All pretty and pink, just the way I love it." I didn't know if his praise should make me feel good—or terrify me. There was something about Damon. All his words had double meanings, or a sinister undertone. I arched my back a little more, feeling the shackles pull at the skin around my wrists.

That slow tongue was back, lapping at my entrance, pushing at the ring, getting me wet.

Getting me ready for his cock.

I couldn't help myself. My knees buckled at the thought of Damon's fat dick splitting my ass. Oh, I'd seen it, all right. Damon had been sunning himself on a towel in his yard, his body oiled and gleaming in the sun. I'd watched him lying there, hand slowly coaxing his cock into fullness. I recalled the heat that flooded through me, heat that had nothing to do with the temperature that summer's afternoon, and *everything* to do with the massive man-meat between Damon's legs.

Man-meat that I wanted to fucking *own* me.

I gave a jolt when Damon slid a finger into my hole, his tongue licking around it. *Fuck, even his fingers are wide.* I bit back my groan when he pulled free, and spat out a low moan of pleasure when *finally*, his tongue explored me, probing me. Damon's hum of satisfaction sent prickles all over my skin.

"Your ass tastes good," he murmured, before diving back in, licking into my hole, forcing his tongue deeper into me. I couldn't keep still. I pushed back, desperate for more. If my hands had been free I would have pushed his face deep into my crack.

And damn it, Damon knew it. The wry chuckle that echoed was proof. "Yeah, you like that, don'tcha?" He began to alternate between his tongue and his finger, each time pushing deeper inside me. I rocked my hips, taking more of him into me. When he added a second finger, I wanted to cry out in triumph. *Yes! More, goddamn it, more.* Damon fingered me, first one finger, then two, then back to one, until I was dancing on his fingers, hips jerking. My cock was rigid against my belly, painting it with sticky trails, leaking constantly.

When two fingers became three, *Christ*, I felt so fucking stretched.

Damon had those three fingers wedged deep in my ass, his hand pumping my dick. "Ever thought about being fisted, Pete?" His deep voice dropped even lower.

Shockwaves ricocheted through me. *Oh my fucking God.* I froze, but the image was there in my head. Me on my back, Damon between my spread legs, his arm buried up to the wrist in my body. I trembled—no, I fucking *shook*.

Instantly those fingers inside me stilled. "Not talking about now," he said quietly, "but *fuck*, just the thought of putting my hand inside you makes me so fucking hard." Slowly he fucked me with his fingers, my hole loosening more with each slow slide. "You an' me, Pete. Fuck, the things I'd love to do to ya. Things I've been *waiting* to do with ya."

My stab of panic had passed. His words were making me hot. Making me want.

"Christ, you're hard. You fucking *like* that idea, don'tcha? Me doing things to ya?" His fingers moved faster, slid deeper, and I trembled with pleasure when he nudged my gland. "*There* we go." His voice brimmed with satisfaction and he stroked over my prostate again and again, until my legs felt like brittle glass and my dick leaked copious amounts of pre-cum. "What you thinking about, Pete? What's your imagination showing ya? Me putting you in my sling and fucking ya? Bending you over my bench and plowing your ass? Or maybe bringing round some of my friends so we can take turns reaming your hole, all night long?"

Oh Jesus. *Jesus*. "D-Damon, Christ, what you're doing to me…"

He growled, the sound coming from somewhere deep. "Fuck, yeah, Pete. I've waited long enough to get you just where I want ya." I groaned when he pulled his fingers out of me, but my disappointment soon fled when my cheeks were pulled roughly apart and his tongue was pushing at my hole, demanding entrance.

I tilted my hips, crying out, my voice quavering. "Oh fucking hell, yeah. Don't stop. Eat my fucking boy pussy!" I let out a brief yip of surprise when he slapped my butt cheek, but thankfully he didn't stop, just kept right on fucking me with his tongue. I rotated my hips and he let me, darting and flickering his tongue in and out of my hole. My breathing quickened. Wet sounds filled the basement as Damon licked and sucked at my hole, until all I could think about was getting his dick inside me. "Please, Damon, now, fuck me now," I begged. I howled with frustration when he stopped and began finger-fucking me once more. "For fuck's sake, Damon, *fuck* me!" My cock was hard and aching, and I knew I couldn't take much more. At this rate, I'd come the minute he was inside me.

Damon gave the head of my cock a thump, the jolt of pain slicing through to my groin and settling in my balls, leaving an uneasy feeling in my gut as I cried out.

"I thought you needed a little reminder of who's in charge," he snapped. I could hear the displeasure rumble in his voice. There was a moment when I knew he'd moved away from me, when I could no longer feel his body heat. Then he was back, and the sound of a foil tearing sent a wave of savage hunger through me. Damon laughed. "Yeah, *that* got your attention." He moved closer, until I could feel the heat pouring off him. "You ready to get split open?"

I was *so* fucking ready. In that moment I was hyper aware of everything: the shackles binding me to the cross, my legs wide; his hands on my ass, spreading me; his latex-covered dick, slick with lube, sliding through my crack; the feel of his pubic hair against my butt and his hot breath on my neck, his breathing as rapid as mine.

Damon pressed the head of his cock against my hole and eased it into me. I shuddered, recalling the wide, flared head I'd seen when I'd spied on him. I whimpered when he pulled free of me, only to let out a sigh of pleasure when he entered me once more, this time inching a little farther into me. He repeated this a few times, and each time I could feel my hole relax more and more, until he was sliding deeper into me. "Fuck, your hole just swallows my dick." He inched all the way into me, until I felt his hips snug against my ass.

Christ, I felt full. "God, you've got a fat dick," I gasped. I swore I could feel every inch of it inside me, stretching me.

"That's it, I'm all the way in." Damon gripped my hips and began to thrust, slowly at first, withdrawing almost completely before sliding back into me. He held me in place and filled me with long, slow strokes of his cock, his breathing quickening a little, clearly audible in the quiet basement. "Christ, Pete, your boy-hole was made to be fucked."

My face heated up at his coarse words, but I was filled with a sense of pride.

"Tell me how it feels," he demanded, picking up speed, his thrusts becoming more fluid as he got into his stride. "Because right now your ass is gripping my cock like a fist."

"Feels good," I blurted out. God, had I *ever* taken a dick that felt this fucking good? "Feels like you... you're splitting my ass in two." Right then Damon shoved into me, hard, and I gasped. "Fuck, you're deep." I struggled to breathe evenly. "God, Damon, not sure I can hold it back. All I want right now is for you to pound my ass with that big fucking cock and make me cum." My whole body *ached* to cum.

Damon let go of my hip and tugged at my balls. "No cumming, remember?" He slid into me, moving faster, burying his dick in me. "Forget what I said. You're fucking tight, and hot, so hot on my cock." Hips snapping, flesh striking flesh, like a slap. "More. I want to hear more about how it feels." A brief flare of pain jolted through me when he slapped my ass.

"Fuck!" I wasn't about to tell him the truth, that no one had *ever* fucked me like this. Fuck, why had I wasted my time with twinks, when all the while this fucking hot *bear* of a man was just next door? "Love it when you're deep. When you—" The words died on my tongue when Damon grabbed me around
the throat and began to fuck me with animalistic abandon, his fingers tightening as his thrusts sped up. The world got a little hazy and sparkly, until I felt sure I was about to pass out. He eased his grip and I gulped in air, my body shaking as he stilled inside me.

Oh my fucking God. How had he known?

Damon seized my hair and yanked my head back. "Like that? Did it feel good?" His gaze bored into me. "Yeah, you liked it. Tell me I'm wrong. Tell me you don't wanna be fucked like a little queer bitch."

I wanted to deny it, but the words wouldn't come.

He let go of my hair and gripping my shoulders, he recommenced fucking me, settling into a solid rhythm. "You feel good… wrapped around… my cock," he grunted, pulling on my shoulders, forcing me back onto his shaft. "You like this… my thick dick… in your ass?"

"Fuck, yeah." His thrusts punched the air from my lungs, his hips slamming into my ass. Damon let go and pushed down on my lower back, tilting my ass higher. *Now* each glide of his cock connected with my gland. "Jesus, yes. *Yes*, Damon, just like that." I wanted more, *craved* more. "Harder."

Damon laughed. "Yeah, *there's* my little slut-boy." He covered me with his body, and I could feel the sweat dripping off him. "Say it again."

"Harder." I raised my voice, which shook as he powered into me, deep and hard. "Oh, Jesus, Mary and Joseph, just like that!" He slowed down and I screamed. "Fuck, no! *Don't fucking stop!*"

Damon didn't change the pace, just kept his thrusts slow and even. It was driving me *crazy*. And that bastard was loving every minute of it. "You like this with all the guys who fuck ya?" he drawled.

"No," I growled, forcing myself to stay calm. "No one has *ever* made me want to beg, like I'm begging you now. Damon, for the love of God, just fuck the shit out of me, okay?"

He held himself so still inside me that I thought for a second I'd really fucked it up. When he finally spoke, his voice sent a cold shiver down my spine, as if he'd let loose the hunger raging inside him.

"You got it."

The next moment I was pushed against the cross. Damon pulled my cheeks apart and began to slam into me with long, earth-shuddering thrusts. Each shove of his cock sent him crashing into me, hammering my ass.

"*Fuck*. Damon, yes, fucking *yes*." I couldn't move, pinned by his body while he ravaged my hole, hips rocking, his rhythm frenetic, energetic—goddamn *perfect*. I trembled as his fingers dug deeper into the fleshy part of my ass, and then howled when he sank his teeth into my shoulder, the pain giving an edge to his fucking that sent me over, my balls tight against my body. *Fuck, no*. My dick throbbed. Electricity rocketed up my spine. *Oh fucking hell, no!* I fought it, clawing to rein in the ecstasy that ripped through me, pulsed inside me in a wave of heat.

Too late. My cock erupted, jetting hot spunk onto the floor, and I sagged against my bonds.

Damon tensed behind me, hands tight on my hips. "Fuck, you're making me cum." He thrust hard and froze.

Oh God. I could *feel* his orgasm, feel his dick pumping cum into the condom, feel his heart beating, his breath on my neck. I groaned, the sound pouring out of me. Damon's head dropped to my shoulder, his breathing harsh and staccato, his cock still twitching inside me. A full body shiver rippled through me as the implications set in.

Oh fuck. Damon was gonna punish me.

My heart pounded when he stirred behind me and reached up to free my wrists from the restraints. He rubbed vigorously over the skin. I stood there, trembling, my mind focused on one thing while he crouched down to unfasten the shackles around my ankles.

What's he gonna do to me?

Finally free, I turned to face him. I took in the rise and fall of his wide furred chest, damp with sweat, his cock, still half-hard, still encased in the condom that was full of his spunk. What unnerved me, however, was his shiteating grin.

Damon shook his head. "Petey-boy, you came all over my nice, clean playroom floor." He folded his arms across his chest.

Shit. "Damon, it... it just felt too fucking good." I struggled to breathe evenly.

Damon stopped my words with a finger across my lips. "On your hands and knees, right now. Clean it up." When I stared at him, that grin widened. "With your tongue."

I shuddered. He was serious. I took a breath, lowered myself onto my knees and brought my head down to the gray vinyl tiles that covered the basement floor.

Could've been worse. Could've been a lot worse.

"Good boy," Damon's voice echoed above me. "Make sure you get it all."

Slowly I lapped up the cold, sticky cum, making sure not one drop remained. By the time I straightened, he'd pulled off the condom and was standing, feet slightly apart, his dick sticky with his jizz, that grin still in evidence. "Now suck my cock." His voice was husky, his shaft already trying to rise.

I crawled closer and waited while he grasped his dick and painted my lips with the sticky fluid. I licked them and then took him into my mouth, running my tongue over the head, before sucking him deeper. He grabbed my hair, his fists so tight that tears burned on my cheeks as he pulled on the strands.

"Fuck, yeah, clean it, pussy boy."

My chest swelled with pride to hear the hitch in his breathing and the hoarse tone in his voice. I sucked hard, feeling his shaft thicken and lengthen in my mouth. *This* was my opportunity to appease him, to make up for my orgasm without permission. *This* was my moment to shine.

I was born to be a cocksucker.

Damon moved his hands to my head and held me steady, thrusting slowly into me, hips rocking gently as he eased his dick deeper into me, until he was fully erect, the head bumping the back of my throat. I thanked God for the lack of a gag reflex and deepthroated him, swallowing around that thick cock, listening to his breathing sharpen and quicken.

"Fucking God," he said weakly.

Yes! I grabbed onto his ass and squeezed hard, pulling him deeper. Damon let out a snarl and started to fuck my face, his fingers taking tight hold of my hair. I relaxed my throat and let him, and it wasn't long before his dick swelled in my mouth and he was coming again, pumping hot cum down my throat. I swallowed hard, taking it all, every last drop, until he was spent. I eased him free and cleaned his cock with my tongue, taking my time, worshiping it.

When I was done, Damon grabbed me under my pits and hauled me to my feet. My mouth was taken in a brutal kiss, sucking on my tongue, my bottom lip. He broke away from me and stepped back, his breathing still uneven. He studied me for a moment, until I was squirming from being under such careful scrutiny.

Damon grinned. "Same time next week?"

AFTER

TANTALUS

AFTER

Damon hasn't had many curveballs thrown his way, and when life manages this, he can usually dodge them.
But not this one.
This one bites him – right in the rear end.

AFTER

Okay, this is a dream.
That wasn't my ceiling up there. Those weren't my drapes. And...

I stopped assessing the furnishings when cool hands spread my ass and a *very* wet tongue licked long and slow over my hole, accompanied by a drawn-out, satisfied hum.

Fuck, that feels good.

As dreams went, this was a damn good one. I didn't have a fucking *clue* who I was dreaming about, but *fuck*, that tongue was working my asshole good. I shuddered as it pushed insistently at my hole, then alternating with a long, broad lick across it. I went to grab my mystery Ass Eater's head to push him deeper into my crack, but....

What the fuck? I was tied down. Wrists. Ankles. My body tensed and I pulled on my restraints, testing them. I twisted my head to look, and saw my wrists handcuffed to the posts. I tried to ease out of them but the metal bit into the delicate skin on my wrist. My legs were allowed some movement, so I guessed there were long straps tethered to the bed posts, cuffs at the end of them. I was still going nowhere, however.

Instantly I was very much awake.

Who the *FUCK* had me in cuffs? I growled.

"What the *fuck* is going on here?" I yelped as someone bit into my ass cheek. "Yow! Cut that out!"

A familiar chuckle. "Good morning." Another chuckle, and then that warm tongue was back, lapping where the teeth had sunk in, soothing away the sting.

"Pete?" My neighbor, Pete? Nah, it couldn't be him. Little fucker didn't have the balls. I strained my neck, trying to see, but *Christ*, that hurt. Somewhere inside my head, something was chipping away at my skull with a rock hammer, and I knew what *that* meant. Too much alcohol the night before. And whoever was down there wasn't helping none, either: it was damn near impossible to think straight while he was lick, lick, licking my ass, pushing his tongue against my pucker. "Fuck, don't stop," I gritted out, pushing down hard, wanting more. *Loved* it when a guy ate my ass. My cock hurt as it throbbed, so flushed with blood I swore it was about ready to pop. I was dripping too, right onto my belly, all that stickiness creating a nice little mess in my body hair.

But I wanted more, *needed* more. Like that guy's face deeper in my crack, that wicked tongue as far in my hole as it would go. I wanted to plant my hands in his hair and fucking *hold* him there, until I shot my load down his fucking throat....

Except I was still tied the fuck down.

"Get me outta these things," I ground out, pulling my wrists against their restraints.

That tongue stopped working its magic. "Unlike a cat, I only have the one life." He cackled. "And I intend to hold on to it." He went right back to rimming my ass.

How the fuck could I stay mad at him when he was doing that? And this time there was no doubt: it *was* Pete.

That was when the teasing started. A slow circle of my hole, so slow that I was close to screaming at him, wanting him to *hurry the fuck up* and fuck me with it. Only he didn't, the little shit. He just kept right on with that damned lap, lap, lapping, until all I wanted was to get my fingers curled in his hair and hold him there till I'd had enough. And all the while my poor, neglected dick was leaking precum in sticky trails across my belly, twitching each time the little fucker dipped his tongue into my hole.

My head was still aching. Had I drunk *that* much last night?

"God, you taste good," Pete whispered, his breath warm against my hole, making my ring contract while little electric prickles danced across my balls. That goddamn tongue flickered in and out of me, so good, nerves endings lighting up like a fucking Christmas tree. He licked a path over my taint, his tongue dragging over my sac, before tracing its way up my hard as steel cock.

"Fuck, yeah." His breath washed over my shaft: the little fuck was panting, teasing my desire with nothing more than his breathing. That was it, someone needed to die, someone with sexy eyes, a chest and abs covered in dark blond hair, and a tight little body that had been calling to me ever since he'd moved in next door. I sucked in a moan when his wet lips claimed my dick head, tongue flicking the slit before he took it deep. I punched up with my cock, wanting more. Pete choked on my girth and it served him right, the scheming little fucker.

"Take it, you little bitch," I growled, thrusting until my dick bumped the back of his throat. Fuck, he just *took* it, his mouth suckling my dick like it was made of honey. I thought he'd gag some more in his eagerness to take my fat cock down his throat, until I remembered that last blow job. Little bastard had no gag reflex. And *Jesus fuck,* that was good, having my cock cuddled by wet heat while he loved on my shaft with his tongue.

Then everything ground to a halt.

"Don't you fuckin' stop now," I howled, my hands clenched into fists, the bite of the cuffs stinging my wrists.

Peter laughed. The little shit *laughed*. "I don't think you're in much of a position to tell me what to do," he drawled. Unhurried fingers trailed down over my sac and along my inner thighs, the touch light. I caught my breath when warm lips brushed over the skin he'd just caressed, soft kisses that I hadn't expected. "And I can do what the fuck I want." A slow tongue over the head of my prick, teasing my slit, followed by a playful bite to my dick. I lifted my head from the pillow, the muscles in my neck taut, and snarled. His eyes were bright with glee. "See? I'm calling the shots. I can take things as slow as I like. All you have to do is lie back and enjoy it."

"I'd enjoy it more if you got the fuck on with it!" I wrenched at my restraints, the bed creaking with the effort. "Now get—" I groaned when his lips tightened around my shaft, mouth like a fucking suction hose as he took me deep. Then the conniving little shit set to fucking *humming*, the vibrations shooting up the length of my dick, until I swore I could feel them in my balls. "Fuck, yeah."

More of that and I was gonna cream, all the way down his tight throat. But every time I pushed deeper, Pete pulled off, the bastard. My jaw ached from me clenching it so tight, and those fucking rock hammers were back at it.

When I get my hands on him, he is so gonna regret this.

He got into a rhythm, his head bobbing over my cock, and I could feel myself getting close, the familiar pressure building inside me, that insane, all-consuming thirst, begging to be sated. *Finally*.

Until he pulled off completely and climbed off the bed. I lifted my head from the pillows to glare at him. He was naked, that ass jiggling as he turned his back to me. *Fuck, that was one plump ass. Just how I like them.* When he finally let me out of those cuffs, I was gonna ream that ass until he was raw.

But right now I had other things on my mind.

"Get that fucking mouth back on my dick," I gritted out. "Don't you leave me hanging, you cock tease." I strained to see what he was doing. "What the fuck are you—"

Something was buzzing.

The mattress dipped as he got back on the bed. "Now hush." Pete knelt between my spread legs, grinning, his cock hard, poking up toward his belly. "Time to slow things down a notch. Can't have you exploding all over yourself just yet." He stretched out his hand toward my chest, those nimble fingers ghosting over a nipple. My muscles rippled, dick jerking while my ass still begged for that nefarious tongue of his.

I craned my neck to see and let rip with a

loud snort. "Is that the best you can do?" My dick ached, my balls ached, all I wanted to do was fucking *cum,* and he was dancing over my nipples with a weeny little bullet vibrator attached to his forefinger. Yeah, it felt good, but I fucking *needed.*

Pete ignored me, running his fingers through my chest hair. "*Love* all this fur," he purred. "So soft, so much of it. And these muscled pecs... I could spend all day licking you from head to foot." The thought of that slow, wicked tongue tracing numerous paths over my skin sent a shiver rippling through me.

He rubbed a hand over my pits, before sliding his fingers over my biceps. "Shit, these arms. You know, I've been dreaming about this body ever since you fucked me." He leaned over me, his face pressed into my pit, inhaling deeply. "You smell so good."

Fuck, I could smell *him*, that heady mix of musk and warm skin infiltrating my nostrils until I was breathing him in.

Pete sat up, his vibrating finger circling my nipple, making it hard. He slid his hand down over my belly, edging closer to my cock. The muscles in my abs danced under his fingers, quivering as he trailed over them, skimming them when I made a noise in the back of my throat. "Patience," he said, smiling. "We're on *my* time, remember? Not yours. Besides, it's Sunday, you got no place to be, and I've plans for this luscious bod." He gently stroked my thigh, dipping toward my groin.

"Stop playing and fucking *do* something," I snarled.

"Like this?" That buzzing moved lower, until he was pressing it under my balls, sending vibrations right through my sac. He applied more pressure to my taint and I felt it all the way along my prick. "Oh, you like that. You're precumming like a leaking faucet." He kept the vibrator where it was and bent over to lap it up.

Fuck. The combination of his tongue to my cockhead and that buzzing to my taint....

"More," I growled. I shuddered when he sucked the head of my dick into his mouth and stroked up and down my shaft with his finger. When the buzzing stopped, I strained against the cuffs. I wanted to grab the little shit around his throat. "You're a fucking little—"

A groan rumbled out of me when something lightly touched my shaft. *Oh my God, what the fuck....* This was bigger, deeper, sending waves of pleasure pulsing through my cock, all the way down to my balls.

"So, you like my Magic Wand?" Pete stroked it up and down my shaft, before rolling it over the ridge under my dick.

"Fuck, that's fierce." I cried out when he held it there and applied pressure to the head, deepening the vibrations. "You're gonna make me cum." I gasped when he slowly stroked it down my shaft to the root, his mouth sucking hard again, tongue pushing into my slit. "Pete, let me cum."

The buzzing stopped but my body was still rocking, my head still spinning—whether from pleasure or the remnants of a hangover, I was too close to the edge to care. I bit back the scream of frustration when the fucker pulled away from my cock, only to have a slick finger sink into my ass. I shuddered at the invasion, my body both welcoming it and fighting it—fuck, when was the last time I'd had *anything* up there? My dildo was stuffed into a drawer, neglected. Who needed it when there were so many willing holes crying out to be fucked? And as for the last time I'd had a dick up my ass, when the fuck was that? Long enough that I couldn't bring it to mind—no, wait...

His face was right there in the forefront of my mind. Michael, my second boyfriend when I was in college, studying Psychology. The first—and only—time I bottomed. The first guy to leave me with a scarred heart—and the last, if I had anything to do with it.

I was brought back to the present when Peter crooked his finger to stroke over my gland, sending waves of pleasure pulsing through me, leaving me gasping.

"Yes!" I pushed down hard, wanting it deeper, chasing my climax. He added another finger, sliding deeper to nudge my gland. I groaned when he withdrew them.

Pete snickered. "Sorry. This is just to prepare you."

Prepare me? If he means what I think he means...God, he wouldn't play with fire like that... Would he? Because if Pete thought he was going to—

I stiffened as something cold spread my ass. Something cold and unyielding that had my hole clamping down on it as it invaded me. "What the fuck, Pete! What the fuck is that?"

"Something fun." Whatever else he'd been about to say was lost when his doorbell rang. "I should probably go get that." Pete clambered off the bed and pulled on a pair of shorts.

What in the fucking name of....?

"Get your ass back here!" I shouted, yanking against my restraints. I was light-headed, sweat popping out on my brow, making my face tingle, my breathing shallow and erratic. I tried to lift my shoulders from the bed but with my arms stretched wide and my wrists cuffed to the bedposts, it was impossible. I snarled. I was gonna fucking *kill* him.

Buzz.

My ass was buzzing. Whatever he'd left in me was fucking *buzzing,* sending pulse after pulse through me. *How the...?*

Realization hit me at the exact moment another bolt of blue fucking lightning buzzed through my hole and zapped up my spine—and for the love of God—made my dick throb like a son of a bitch.

The little bastard had a remote.

I closed my eyes, head still aching, the vibrations in my ass driving me crazy. How in the hell had I gotten into this? More awake now, I recalled the previous night, my memories less hazy. Looking over the hedge that lay between our properties, intrigued by the smell of barbecue and the sound of laughter. *The pool party.* Semi-naked guys lounging around Pete's pool, drinking, diving into the water, lying on towels and loungers. Pete inviting me to join them. Alcohol. A hell of a lot of alcohol. I'd been that drunk, I'd staggered through the house in search of a bathroom, which had turned out to be occupied. Pete's bedroom. Pete's bathroom. Collapsing onto Pete's bed. Drunken oblivion.

I groaned loudly, the sound reverberating

through my aching head. That thing in my ass kept switching programs, pulses one minute, a slow, low vibration the next, then onto another variation. My cock was pointing up to the ceiling, precum sliding down over the head, twitching every time the program changed.

When the buzzing moved up a level, I felt the vibrations from my toes to my head and all points in between. They tingled through my dick, shooting down into my balls. All I wanted was to sink my dick into Pete's ass and shoot my load.

"Sorry about that." Pete was back at the bedside, grinning. "I forgot I'd loaned Frank my garden shears. He was just bringing them back."

Garden shears? Was he fucking *kidding*? "You left me like this to go get a pair of *garden shears*?" That was fucking *it*. Pete's ass had a date with my paddle.

He tut-tutted and held up the small black plastic remote. "Aw, are you not having fun yet?" There was a wicked gleam in his eyes. "Maybe I should just leave it on random."

"You little shit," I ground out. "Just you wait until I—" I howled as he pressed a button on the remote and the vibrating whatever sent waves through my prostate.

"Aw, is that too much?" Pete crooned. His fingers moved and the level dropped. I groaned as he pulled the vibrator from my ass. "That better?" He snickered.

I panted, my chest heaving. "Payback is a bitch. Remember that."

Pete ignored my threat and glanced toward my dick, licking his lips. "Would you look at that." He shucked off his shorts and dived back onto the bed, settling on his belly between my legs and tugging my aching shaft lower until it was in his mouth. He worked the head, rolling his tongue around it, and I rocked my hips, not pushing too far for fear he'd pull off and decide to employ that rocket up my ass again.

Pete paused and lifted his head to grin at me. "You're learning."

The fucking nerve....

My retort was forgotten when he went back to sucking my dick like a starving man. I breathed faster, my orgasm now almost in sight, balls tight. "Go on," I urged him. "That's it, just like that." I rolled my hips, thrusting a little deeper, hands clenched into fists. Pete sucked harder until he was deepthroating again, shifting position so he was poised above my cock. I ached to reach down and grab his head, just hold him there so I could skullfuck him.

Pete raised his head, his lips dripping with saliva, and gasped. "Fuck, you've got a fat dick."

I groaned. "And you've stopped again."

Pete's grin was beginning to worry me. "That's because I'm not ready to let you come yet." He knelt up, that cock still hard and wet-tipped. "I need to slow you down a bit." He peered around him before leaning over me, his fingers stroking along my shaft. When he grabbed my balls and pulled gently on them, I groaned in frustration. It wasn't until I felt the cool metal touch my dick that I realized what he was doing.

A fucking cock ring.

He'd eased my balls through it and now it circled my cock around the base. My dick was rigid, dark with blood. Pete stared at it, lips parted.

"Now that is a thing of beauty." He lowered his head until the tip kissed his lips, before tracing the thickened vein that ran along the side with his tongue. A shudder ran the length of me. I was so close.

Pete shifted until he was on all fours, kneeling over me. "So how does it feel, Damon? Hmm? To be helpless? Restrained? So close to cumming you can almost taste it?" He bent down and flicked my nipple with his tongue, sending more shivers through me. He smiled against my chest and did it again, only this time he stroked between my nipples where the hair was at its most dense. "You said payback is a bitch. Well, what do you call this, if not payback for last week?"

"I won the bet, remember?" I flung back at him. "I got to do whatever I wanted. You agreed." I stifled a moan as he took a nipple between his teeth and tugged on it. "And I... didn't hear you... complaining when... I was... fucking that tight little... hole of yours with my fat cock." He didn't let up for a second, flicking and sucking, licking, biting, the sensual onslaught pushing me ever closer to my climax. *That's it, Petey-boy. Just keep doing what you're doing and fucking let me* cum.

Pete lifted his chin and met my gaze. "And just how tight is *your* ass, Damon? Shall we find out?"

What the fuck?

He dipped his head again and kissed my belly, his lips soft against my skin. More kisses, Pete moving lower, until he reached my pubes. "Fuck, you smell even better here." He buried his nose in the crease where groin met thigh. A pause, followed by another slick finger in my ass, only this

Damon & Pete: Playing with Fire

time he slid it in all the way to the knuckle in one long push. I tightened my body around the invader.

Peter looked up at me. "Remind me. What was that you said to me?" He frowned. "Now, what was it exactly?" His brow smoothed out and he beamed at me. "Oh yeah, I remember now. 'You're not gonna be able to use this hole for a week.'" That evil grin revealed him for the horny little devil that he was. He withdrew his finger, reached behind him and when he straightened, my asshole tightened at the sight of the long, thick, veiny dildo in his hand. Pete waggled it in front of me, still grinning, and *shit*, I swore there were icy fingers dancing up and down my spine.

I lifted my head from the pillow. "Oh no, you fucking don't." I tried to bring my legs together, but Pete pushed with his knees to spread me, insinuating his body between them. The little shit was stronger than he looked.

He dropped the dildo onto the bed and leaned over me, his faces inches from mine, hands gripping my biceps. "You're not fooling me, alright? You bitch and whine, sure, but don't think I don't know how much you like it when I suck you off. It's not like I'm *raping* ya, is it? That dick of yours doesn't lie." He let go of my arm to stroke his fingers along my cock. I shivered, pushing into his touch, and Pete grinned. "So should I stop what I'm doing?" He wrapped his hand around my shaft and I fucked his fist, the precum making everything slippery.

I could have said, 'Yes.' I could have yelled at him to take the cuffs off. But I didn't.

Pete let go of my dick and brought his hands to my chest, him gazing down at me with those sexy as fuck eyes. "Look, it's gonna happen, so why not just lie there and enjoy it?" he whispered, before bringing his lips to my neck and kissing me there. I couldn't help the shiver that ran the length of my body. My neck had always been a sweet spot: my first BF had soon discovered how fast he could turn me on when he nibbled, sucked and licked me there, quickly reducing me to a puddle of goo.

No way was I going to let Pete know the effect his mouth was having on me.

I didn't have to say a word—my cock did all the talking. Pete's lips slid down my neck, soft as anything, and my dick jerked up toward my belly, precum descending from the slit in a stream. I rolled my hips, so fucking aroused it wasn't true, and when Pete called a halt to his sensual torture, his face once more hovering above mine, I knew what was coming. Slowly he descended, lips parted, and although I could have snarled and denied him, I didn't.

His mouth closed over mine and fuck, it was good. I'd expected him to be gentle, but that kiss was anything but. He thrust his tongue deep into my mouth, moaning into it while he claimed my lips, our teeth clashing as I allowed him to take what he wanted. He sucked my bottom lip between his teeth, biting it, before sucking at my tongue. All I yearned for was to have my hands free so that I could grab hold of his head and deepen that kiss, give as good as I got.

When he broke away, panting, his chest heaving, I wanted to growl and tell him to get the fuck back.

Pete sat up and retrieved the dildo. A soft

click and there he was, slicking it with lube. I gazed at it, swallowing at the sight of the wide head, the thickness of it—the length of it. My stomach churned when he slid a couple of fingers back inside me, his eyes focused on my face.

I sucked in a deep breath and stared him down. "You think I've never taken a dick before? You think you're getting payback by fucking me with a *dildo*?" I snorted. "Bring it on."

Pete was still for a moment, his fingers at rest deep in my ass. "You got it." He withdrew them and rubbed the dildo over my hole, smacking it against my pucker, the sound slick and loud. I held my breath as he positioned the silicone cock against my hole, exerting slight pressure so I knew it was there, cool and blunt. Then slowly he pushed, his gaze locked onto the glistening shaft that was sliding into my ass.

Christ, I felt that. It stretched me, splitting my ass wide, every ridge and vein touching me as it made its way deeper. "Fuck, gonna feel that in my throat if you push it any farther," I gasped out. Pete said nothing, his attention still fixed on where he was penetrating me with that pink monster. "Who the fuck did they model this on? King Kong?" It was like being shafted with a length of two by four.

That drew a grin from him. "No—Jeff Stryker."

A groan rumbled out of my depths. "Figures. You a size queen, Petey-boy?" I clenched around the mass that was invading my body, relaxing when Pete slowly eased it out of me. I could still feel it, though.

That grin didn't alter one bit as he reached out and grasped my dick, sliding his hand from root to tip. "What do you think?"

That was it, I'd lost it. I was tied to my neighbor's bed while he slowly slid a dildo into me, and yet what was I doing? Feeling proud that he appreciated the size of my cock.

Any further such reflections were swept from my mind when Pete slid the dildo back inside me with one long push and began to fuck me with it, picking up a little speed.

"Relax," Pete said, his hand rubbing over my belly before he wrapped it around my cock. "It feels better if you relax." His hand sure felt better where it was.

The fucking irony....

I stifled my groans as he filled me to the hilt. "Do... do you know what... I do for a living?" I forced myself to relax, the burn starting to ebb away.

Pete watched me, lips parted, his arm moving as he continued to fuck me with the dildo, moving faster, pushing it into me more firmly. "No," he whispered. "Fuck, look at you." His focus was my cock, a rigid pole of flesh, dark and throbbing.

I grinned, hips rocking as I started to push down on the silicone *log* he was shoving into me with greater speed. "I'm a sexologist." I arched my back, the friction building inside my hole, making me burn with need. "I advise people... on their sex lives."

Pete widened his eyes. "Oh, we are gonna have to talk about this, but not now." He pushed the dildo into me, until I felt its balls against my ass. "I have something much more important to do."

I had to agree. "Yeah, like bring me off." I glared at him, tugging against the cuffs. "Why the fuck have you stopped again? What you gonna do now—leave me here while you go make yourself a coffee?"

That wicked grin flashed across his face before he reached behind him yet again. A tearing sound and then I was thanking God when Pete covered my aching cock with a condom. He swiped a slick hand over my rigid shaft. "Yeah, that got your attention, didn't it? Not complaining now, are you? Not now you see what's coming."

My ass was still stretched, full of that fucking silicone beast. "You just gonna leave it in me?"

Pete nodded, shifting until he was astride me, his ass so hot against my dick. He knelt up, reaching behind him, and *Jesus*, I wanted to see. Wanted to watch him sink those fingers into his own ass as he got himself ready for my cock, his hole glistening and pink like I remembered it. Remembered sinking my dick into that tight little hole, while he hung from my St. Andrew's cross...

Christ, was that only a week ago?

He pulled his asscheeks apart and I pushed up, sliding my shaft through that furry crack. Pete rolled his hips sinuously, his breathing speeding up as the head of my dick rubbed over his hole. "C'mon," I groaned. In that moment the cuffs were all but forgotten. Fuck, I wanted in.

He grabbed my shaft and there it was, that hot little hole, just *begging* for me to thrust up into it. I gritted my teeth, rocking up off the mattress impatiently. Pete tightened his grip on my dick and locked eyes on me.

"This is mine for the morning, you got that?"

I snorted. "Only because I can't get my hands on you."

He smiled. "I've been thinking about this all week, ever since you fucked me. Thinking about how I could get this gorgeous cock in my ass again." He cocked his head. "You got any idea what it did to me, watching you stretched out in your back yard, this furry bod all glistening with sweat while you played with yourself?" He tugged on my dick before reaching lower to squeeze my balls.

I growled. "When I get outta these cuffs...." My ass clenched and I groaned as it tightened around the solid mass he'd left in there.

Pete pulled a face. "Aw, poor Damon. At least I'm gonna be nicer than you were to me."

"What does that mean?"

He grinned, holding my cock steady against his hole, and leaned forward to whisper. "You won't get punished for cumming." Then he rocked back and sank down onto my rod, impaling himself and burying my dick balls deep in the tightest ass I'd ever known.

"Jesus *fuck*!" The speed of it left me gasping. Shit, every inch of my cock was in that snug little hole. "Goddamn, that feels fucking good." I shuddered when he slowly lifted himself up, my hands clenching into tight fists at the sight of him. My fingers ached to be pressing into his hips while I brought him down *slam* onto my cock. But all the breath whooshed out of me when he sat back down and I filled him to the hilt.

"God, yes," he moaned, rocking on top of

me, hips rotating while he fucked himself on my shaft. His cock was like stone, a solid arrow pointing to the ceiling, leaking copious amounts of precum. God, I wanted to touch it. I planted my feet flat on the mattress, legs spread, and tilted my hips to fuck up into him, moving with him. "Yeah, like that," he shouted, leaning back into it, the long line of his body stretched out, belly taut, nips hard little nubs standing proud. He grabbed my thighs and balanced himself while I thrust into him, his head thrown back.

Fuck, the heat of him, searing my dick, his body wrapped around it so tight, so snug, that I wanted to lose myself in the sensations for fucking *ever*. My hips rocked up faster, my body hurtling toward the orgasm I knew was imminent. This was it, finally, after being so fucking close....

Pete pulled himself upright and stared at me, his upper body still while he rolled his hips fluidly, undulating on my cock, so goddamn sensual that I couldn't take my eyes off of him. He reached behind him and I groaned when he tugged at the dildo, just enough that I felt it. Pete shoved it back into me, panting. "How's that feel?" His chest gleamed with sweat. "You like that? Me fucking your hole while you fuck mine?" He moved his hand faster, the dildo slamming farther into me as I fucked him harder, shoving up into him, hips snapping.

"Fuck, yeah," I gasped. I couldn't deny how amazing it felt. I didn't want it to stop.

Except that was when lightning zapped down my spine into my balls and I shot my load into the condom. I pushed my head back into the pillow, mouth wide, straining against my bonds while my balls emptied themselves into the latex. My whole body tingled, heat pulsing through me as I pulsed cum into him. The muscles in my thighs trembled and my belly quivered, my ass clenching around the dildo that was still wedged inside my hole.

Pete shivered, hands on my chest, his head bowed. "I feel that. Fuck, I feel your dick throbbing inside me." He rocked slowly, bending lower, his mouth *right there* and I took it, welcoming the kiss. I eased down, moving with him, my tongue between his lips, savoring the taste of him while my cock pulsed the last of my cum into the condom. Pete returned the kiss, still hungry for it, moaning softly into it as his movements grew less frantic. Tiny bursts of electricity jolted through me, the last of my orgasm, and I lay quiet, my dick still inside him, the dildo in me.

Slowly, Pete lifted himself off of my still half-hard cock, and a sigh shuddered out of him. I glanced at his dick. Even in my restrained condition, I prided myself on being a generous lover. I'd just shot my load, after all. "You haven't come. Want some help with that?"

He nodded, and clambered off me. I lay still, biding my time, anticipating my freedom. I'd give him his climax—that was only fair, he'd worked me up into one hell of an orgasm—but then all bets were off. I was already planning my revenge, starting with a paddling he wouldn't forget in a hurry. And that was nothing compared to what else I had in store for him.

Only he didn't unlock the cuffs.

"Pete?" I pulled against the restraints, the

muscles in my arms and legs tensed. "Come on, you've had your fun. Get me out of these. And get that dildo out of my ass."

Pete moved until he was kneeling once more between my spread legs. He removed the condom and bent over my cock, cleaning it with his tongue. I shuddered, the head sensitive as always. When he took me into his mouth, I groaned. "I'd forgotten what a good little cocksucker you are." My dick was already taking an interest. "You could do that when I'm out of the cuffs, you know." Yeah, with my hands on his head while I fucked his mouth good and hard.

He gave my cockhead a final lick. "Let me deal with this first." The feel of his fingers on my shaft and balls as he eased the cock ring off, was yet more inducement to send the blood heading south.

"Okay, now the cuffs?" His reluctance to remove them was beginning to worry me.

Pete lifted his head and something in my belly rolled over at the sight of that evil fucking grin. My breathing quickened when he held up another condom packet. "I'm not done yet," he said, eyes gleaming.

I laughed out loud in relief. "Christ, Petey-boy, even I can't work miracles. You might have to wait a while until I get it up again."

Pete shook his head. "It's not for you." He tore open the wrapper—and gloved up his own granite cock. "Now it's my turn." My stomach grew taut as he slowly pulled the dildo from my ass. Pete's grin widened. "You're nice and stretched for me." He smacked his heavy dick against my still aching balls, and I winced. "Not that I'll last all that long once I'm inside you." He shifted closer, hands on my thighs, spreading me wider, until I felt the head of his cock against my loosened hole. "You're slick in there, ready for me."

I tensed, muscles tightened, until it hit me. *It's going to happen, so don't waste energy fighting it. Because when he's done...* Revenge would be so fucking *sweet.*

Not to mention the part of me that had liked how the dildo had felt. Like I'd tell *him* that.

I locked eyes with him. "If you're gonna fuck me, then get on with it." I flashed him my coolest smile. "Just be prepared for the consequences."

Pete's smile tightened. "Too late. I've already sold my soul to the Devil." He gripped my thighs and slowly, so fucking slowly, entered me in one long, smooth thrust, closing his eyes as he bottomed out. "Oh my fucking God, how you feel…"

All notions of revenge fled my mind as my attention focused on the dick that was filling me, because *Damn*, it felt good. Peter began a slow in and out motion, his thrusts deep and even. He leaned over me, arms locked at the elbow as he rocked into me, his lips parted, his breath warm on my face. It was slow, gentle, careful, even tender—and the pace was killing me.

I didn't want slow and gentle. I wanted to be *fucked.* I wanted to still be feeling it next fucking week.

I clenched my ass tight around his dick, bearing down as he thrust into me, purposefully driving him toward the edge. I spread my legs as wide as the restraints would allow, so that he got deeper. But still he kept up that unhurried pace, hips rolling, his eyes focused on my face, his breathing rapid. And *Christ*, the friction...

Then I got it. This was more payback. Hadn't I teased him just like this, until he'd begged me to fuck him?

Fuck it. If it got me what I wanted, what I *needed*—me out of those cuffs, Pete over my knee and me paddling his bare ass—then I'd beg.

"Fuck me," I demanded. "Come on, Pete, *plow* that ass. Fuck me like you mean it." I glared at him. "You got what you wanted, right? Me at your mercy, unable to resist?" I yanked at the cuffs. "See? I'm going nowhere, so why don't you just pound my hole like you know you want to?"

Pete stilled inside me, and the silence that followed had all the hairs on the back of my neck standing up, and shivers tripping the light fantastic up and down my spine. He covered me with his body, sweat dripping off of him onto my chest, and pressed his forearms into the pillows on either side of my head. His face was barely inches away from mine.

"And what if that's not what I want?" The quietly uttered words were followed by a kiss that was nothing like the earlier brutal collision of lips, teeth and tongues. This was slow, deliberate, an exploration, while he began a languid stroking of his cock in and out of my ass with long, even thrusts. Only now the head of his dick was sliding over my gland. Every. Fucking. Time.

Each nudge over that spot sent wave upon wave of pleasure crashing through me, making my cock jerk against my belly. His skin was damp, his sweat mingling with my own, making everything slicker.

"*This* is what I want," Pete whispered against my mouth. "I don't want to hammer your ass in one frenetic thrust after another." His hips rocked into me just that little bit faster, losing his rhythm as he picked up the pace. "I want to feel everything, every inch of you around my dick as I fuck you." Faster, thrusting harder, going deeper. Pete's breathing became shallow, escaping in short bursts. He grabbed hold of my shoulders, anchoring himself while he fucked me, eyes still locked on mine.

I wanted to whine at him, snarl, tell him to get the fuck on with it, but those sweet waves of pleasure were rippling through me, sending a rush of heat spreading to my extremities. My toes curled, my arms were taut, the muscles tensed, my belly hard, and still he pushed me closer to another climax. His fingers dug into my shoulders, deep into the flesh, providing a welcome edge of pain.

That was better. That was what I knew, what I could deal with. "Come on, come on," I urged him, as he began to piston-fuck me, hips snapping. Pete groaned, body stiffening as he thrust deep inside me. I felt it all the way through me, reverberating deep into my balls, zapping along my cock. Spunk shot from my dick, a couple of spurts that hit my abs and were instantly smeared over both of us when Pete's body sank onto mine, his head dropping to my shoulder.

His breathing was harsh and loud in my ear, brief twitches shaking him while he throbbed inside me, the sweat on my skin cooling. I lay beneath him, my own tremors ebbing away, feeling his body move with each rise and fall of my chest. That longed-for satiation spread through me in a slow current as my breathing and heartbeat returned to their normal pattern.

It wasn't long, however, before he shifted position, his cock slipping from my hole as he sat up, the condom white with his cum. He leaned over toward the nightstand and the next thing I knew, my wrists were freed. Pete got down from the bed and unlocked the cuffs from around my ankles. He rubbed the skin briskly, his gaze flickering toward my face. "Are you okay? No numbness or anything?"

His concern took the edge off my desire for immediate retribution. "Yeah, no harm done." I sat up and glanced at my chest and belly, sticky with sweat and cum. The first thought to flash through my mind was to make him clean it up with his tongue. That got me smiling. A fitting punishment that would definitely do for starters.

Before I could utter a word, Pete walked around to the side of the bed and lowered himself to his knees. He bowed his head, hands behind his back. "I'm ready for my spanking now."

For a moment I gaped at him, overtaken by the unexpected turn of events. When he lifted his chin and grinned at me, I quickly regained my composure. I got off the bed and stood in front of him, arms folded across my damp chest, feet planted wide, my cock still sticky with cum. I stared down at him, not believing the contrite posture for one second.

"You think you're gonna get away with a spanking?" I snorted. "Boy, that's just the beginning."

His eyes flashed. "I was sort of counting on it—Sir."

Looks like somebody wants to play. I grinned. Pete had just opened up a big can of whoopass.

CONSEQUENCES

TANTALUS

CONSEQUENCES

Pete knew there'd be payback and he's ready to take his punishment. But what Damon comes up with is *so* not what he expected...

CONSEQUENCES

I took another look at my watch. Seven o'clock. *Where the fuck is he?* Damon's text had been specific: *six-thirty, the back alley past Montgomery Street, wait by the red dumpster.* Don't. Be. Late. The incongruity was the instruction to come smart-casual. *To do what? Hang around in an alley?*

Not that I was all *that* worried. I doubted we'd be staying there long. Damon had to have some other destination up his sleeve, right? Maybe he intended taking me to some sleazy, kinky club where all the men wore leather boots and caps and little else, their feet propped up on the backsides of their slaves who knelt, buck naked, oiled and collared...

Fuck. Talk about my mind running away with me. *Get a grip, Pete.* Still, it was a great image, the thought of leather daddies in assless chaps, their rigid dicks receiving exquisite tongue attention from their naked boys...

There I went again, my dirty little mind shifting into overdrive.

You don't know what he has planned. Come on, this is Damon, *for Christ's sake.* The same Damon who'd let me stew for *three fucking weeks.* One minute I was kneeling beside my bed, expecting the wrath of Damon to descend, anticipating whatever evil, raunchy payback he had in mind for my little scheme, and the next? His phone rang, he leaped up and grabbed his clothes from where I'd left them on the chair, and then he was out the door. I'd spent the rest of the day waiting for the ax to fall, but heard nothing. Then I'd found the note he'd shoved into my letter box, telling me he'd be away for a while, and would I water his yard?

Water his fucking *yard*? Really?

That certainly didn't feel like payback. 'A while' had turned into three weeks, with not a single word from him. But yeah, you can bet I'd watered his yard.

I wouldn't have dared do otherwise. Though it *was* tempting to use my dick as the hose. I didn't, of course. Because if Damon had come home to find all his plants dead and the yard stinking of piss, I think I'd have ended up six feet under it.

Another glance at my watch. Twenty seconds later than the last time I looked at it. But after another ten minutes and still no Damon, I started to get antsy. I mean, standing in an alley, dressed in chinos, a button-down shirt and a jacket, the air filled with mouthwatering smells, pumped out of nearby vents...

The sound of a door opening grabbed my attention. *At last.*

Only, it wasn't Damon.

A guy in a white tunic and checkered pants stuck his head around the door. "You Pete?" From behind him came the clatter and noise of what had to be a very busy kitchen.

I nodded warily.

"Well, get your ass in here. You don't want to be late, do ya?"

Late? Late for what?

I didn't wait around to be asked again. I stepped past him into a bright hallway, boxes and crates piled neatly behind the door. He beckoned for me to follow him and we turned right into a large restaurant kitchen, bustling with at least ten people, and that didn't include the servers who darted in and out of the swing doors, dressed in black and armed with trays.

"Wait there."

I did as instructed, flattening my body against the wall to stay out of everyone's way. The place was a hive of activity: dishes being prepared and placed under hot lamps, dirty dishes being piled into sinks full of hot water, sauces being poured, vegetables chopped, pans stirred...

When a dark-haired guy in a smart gray suit appeared, it was obvious he was Someone: heads turned in his direction and voices were lowered. He glared at the assembled workers.

"Right, Donny's in charge, and you'd better make sure *every single frigging plate* is goddamn perfect, you hear me? Because tonight I'll be one of the customers, and if I see so much as a spinach leaf out of place, I will come down on you like God Allfrigging Mighty when this shindig is over, you got that?"

"Got it, chef." The phrase echoed around the tiled kitchen, heads bobbing nervously.

He gave them one last baleful stare before turning to gaze at me. "Right, let's get outta here. Damon's waiting for you upstairs." He led me out into the restaurant, where a piano played softly and customers spoke in low voices over candlelit tables. Disappointment welled up inside me as we weaved through them. A goddamn restaurant. *So much for a leather club*. It looked like the only thing in the cards tonight was dinner. *Dinner? What the fuck kind of payback is that?* We reached the front desk, where a sharp turn left revealed a staircase covered in red carpet, at the top of which was…

Damon, leaning against the wall, his gaze focused on me.

Holy fuck.

Damon waited beside a closed door, wearing an expensive-looking dark blue suit and white shirt open at the collar, a white handkerchief peeking out of his breast pocket. I resisted the urge to lick my lips.

The chef walked ahead of me up the stairs and stopped in front of him. "He's all yours. Don't be too long. You know how she gets." He flashed a grin in my direction.

That was when I saw it. The resemblance. I only had to look at those two together to know the chef had to be Damon's brother. A little younger, sure, but no doubt about it. *What the fuck?*

He pulled open the door and disappeared, leaving me standing there with Damon.

Now what?

Damon looked me up and down in silence, which got my heartbeat racing.

"Hey." Any smart-ass remarks I'd planned flew out of my head at the sight of him, because fuck, he looked downright gorgeous.

He regarded me with a smile. "You'll do."

"Gee, thanks." I glared at him. "Now tell me what I'll do for?" I glanced at my casual attire. Next to Damon, I felt unkempt.

He doesn't seem to think so, does he?

I gave an internal snort. *That's because he's read the script. He knows what's coming.*

"I get that you have questions," he said calmly, "but guess what? I'm not about to answer any of 'em. All you need to know is you owe me after that dirty stunt you pulled, and this is where I collect. Some of it, at least." He pointed to the door. "Through there."

"Aren't you going to tell me what I'm walking into?" I wasn't panicking, but that surge of disappointment was back. Ever since his text had arrived that morning, I'd been fantasizing about this. Where we'd go. What we'd do. Scrap that—what *he'd* do to *me*. The way I figured it, we were about to have dinner, possibly with Damon's brother, and that wasn't exactly a scary prospect. Definitely not *my* idea of payback either.

Damon snorted. "This is all you're getting. You're my date tonight, and it's my mom's sixtieth birthday." He pushed open the door. "And now get in there."

His date? His *mom*?

Jesus fucking Christ, I'm a dead man walking here.

I quickly pulled myself together. *How bad can it be?*

He stood aside to let me enter. I stepped into the warm room and my jaw dropped.

In the center of the room, all the tables had been pushed together to form one huge table, around which sat about thirty people, chatting, laughing and drinking. There were old folks yapping and little kids darting around, making a racket. A table set up under the window was piled high with brightly wrapped gifts, and there were balloons everywhere. Music with a Latin rhythm played in the background, and overall the atmosphere was nothing like the elegant restaurant downstairs. This was louder, brasher, livelier.

It was a freaking family get-together, and I'd just walked in as Damon's date. *Shoot me now.*

Me meeting the BF's parents—it *never* went well. I know at twenty-eight, I'd not had the experience all that often, but yeah, every freaking time it ended up being a dreadful occasion. *This night has all the hallmarks of a disaster waiting to happen, and Damon isn't even my boyfriend.*

"You gonna introduce this pretty boy, Damon?"

I stared at the speaker, an older man in a wrinkled brown suit who was eyeing me like I was the entrée. It gave me the creeps.

Damon stared too, eyebrows arched. "Uncle Ed, this is Pete. And keep your paws off of him, he's mine." He winked at me before grabbing my arm and leading me around the table. Judging from the looks and comments we were getting, I wasn't expected. By the time we reached the head of the table, the air was buzzing with chatter.

"Hey, Mama, happy birthday." Damon bent over to kiss his mom's cheek. When he straightened, I was caught, pinned by a pair of dark brown eyes so like Damon's it was uncanny.

"And who's this?" Her voice was loud. She squinted at me, before reaching into her capacious purse to pull out a pair of glasses. When she put them on, she regarded me so intently that my heart pounded even harder.

"This is Pete, Mama." I waited for him to say

more, but the bastard clammed up, his eyes gleaming as he glanced at me. It was then that I got it.

He's leaving me to sink or swim. He's gonna be no help whatsoever. The fucker.

She lifted her penciled brows. "And who is Pete when he's at home?"

"I'm Damon's next-door neighbor, ma'am," I said politely.

His mama slowly raised her head to look at her son. "Mm-hmm." It was easy to see who Damon got his attitude from. This was no sweet little old lady. Damon's mama was a sharp operator.

Yeah, tonight was going to be terrifying.

His mama looked me up and down, and my heartbeat went into overdrive. One glance at the people assembled told me there was some money in this room: their clothing had that expensive air about it. In my chinos, shirt and old jacket, I was feeling distinctly under dressed.

She speared me with an intense stare. "Damon's neighbor? Then you two aren't dating?"

I jerked my head up to look at Damon, silently pleading for some guidance here. The fucker didn't even look in my direction. He called out a name and left me standing there while he walked around the table to hug some woman in an elegant dress.

I was on my own, apparently.

"No, ma'am. We're not dating." Never mind what Damon had said. Damon was elsewhere.

Up went those penciled eyebrows again. "You're not dating, yet he brings you to my birthday party. I see." She smirked. "So are you doing him or is he doing you?"

Christ Almighty. Definitely *not* a sweet little old lady. I nearly choked. There was no fucking way

I was about to answer *that* question. From across the room Damon snuck a peek at me and I glared at him. *When this is over…*

"So, Pete, what do you do?" she asked in a pleasant tone, like butter wouldn't melt and she hadn't just a few seconds ago asked me if her son and I were fucking.

I recovered quickly, silently swearing massive vengeance on my bastard of a neighbor.

"I'm a landscape gardener."

"Oh." She smiled. "That must be interesting. Have you done any work on Damon's yard?"

I glanced across the room at him and caught his attention. He raised a wine glass to me, and I smirked. "Yes, ma'am. I pollinated his flowers for him," I said in a loud voice.

Damon nearly spat out the mouthful of wine he'd just taken. His mom, however, laughed out loud.

I decided to play nice, even if Damon wasn't. "You have a very large family, Mrs. Ramos," I said politely.

Her eyes lit up. "They're wonderful. Every year I get taken out for dinner by my children and their families. I've celebrated my birthday in some of the finest restaurants in San Francisco, but this is my favorite, for obvious reasons."

I got that, if her son was the chef here. I gazed at the people nearest to her. "And is Mr. Ramos here?"

Her smile faltered. "We lost my husband three years ago, to a heart attack."

"I keep telling her she should find herself a toy boy." Damon strolled over, his important conversation apparently over. His gaze met mine.

"She's still young enough to find someone to pollinate *her* flowers." He waggled his eyebrows.

His mama batted him on the arm. "Hush, you. We're not talking about that again. And I'm not done here. Go talk to someone. I want to talk to Pete." Damon laughed but did as instructed. She patted the empty chair next to her. "Sit here."

Like I could refuse. I sat down between her and Damon's brother, my heart quaking.

"Tell me about yourself. Do you have family here in San Francisco?"

"No, ma'am. My mom died of lung cancer about six years ago, and my dad went not long after her."

Her eyes widened. "No brothers or sisters?"

"No, ma'am." In spite of my nerves, I had to admit the atmosphere in the room was great. *It must be nice to be part of a large family.*

An explosive snort next to me had me turning. Damon's brother huffed. "Think yourself damn lucky. When this pack gets together, anything goes." He extended a hand. "I'm Max, Damon's brother."

I shook it. "The resemblance is uncanny."

Max grinned. "You should have seen Papa. Damon is the spitting image of him."

"Is he the oldest?"

Max nodded. "I'm three years younger."

"And you're the chef here."

He gave me a wry smile. "Some nights, yeah. Other nights I run my restaurant."

Fuck. "I'm sorry, I didn't realize this was your place."

Max didn't appear perturbed. "Why would you? We've only just met." His gaze flashed in

Damon's direction. "It's not like Damon told us he was bringing a guest either."

His mom cleared her throat. "Are we going to be eating any time soon? My stomach thinks my throat's been cut."

Max's laugh was loud and raucous. "Yeah, Mama, real subtle." He addressed the room's occupants. "Okay, people. Take your places, please, so they can start bringing in the first course." He got up and kissed his mom on the cheek.

She chuckled as he walked over to the door. "He's always the same. He's left the manager in charge downstairs, but will he let him do his job?" Around them everyone hurried to take their places around the table, parents settling their children, the noise level gradually dying down.

"You've survived then." Next to me Damon let out a dry chuckle. "Looks like you didn't need me after all."

No way was he off the hook yet.

"Nice of you to warn me," I hissed. "Seriously? Meeting your entire family?"

Damon grinned. "You haven't met them all yet. Wait until dinner's over."

It was going to be a long night.

I had the feeling the evening was drawing to a close. When I peered at my phone, I got a shock. It was getting on for eleven o'clock. *Christ, these people can talk.*

I'd had my share of conversation for the night. Damon had introduced me to his siblings, and *that* had been quite the education. I guessed Damon's parents had instilled in all their six kids an admirable work ethic. His sister Martella owned a very swanky hair salon in Sausalito. Lauren—she was the one elegantly dressed—had a dress shop near Fisherman's Wharf. Leo owned a car dealership downtown. The baby of the family was Paula: at twenty-five, she'd just finished law school and was working in a successful law firm. They were all friendly and polite toward me, all of them engaging me in conversation at some point during the evening.

Paula seemed the most at ease. We chatted about her studies and her ambitions to rise up within the law firm. When a natural lull in the conversation occurred, she leaned back on her chair and sought out Damon. "Well, *I'm* gonna ask, seeing as none of this lot have had the guts. What's going on, bro? You never bring a date to these affairs. Why start now?" She gave him a sweet smile. "Is there something going on we should know about?" She didn't seem to care that I was seated close by.

Damon fired her what could only be described as a warning glance, but she met his stare with one of her own, clearly not about to budge. He chuckled. "Nope, nothing going on, sis." His gaze latched onto mine for a moment, before he went back to his conversation with Max.

Paula arched her eyebrows. "I see." I was trying not to smirk and carried on talking to Leo, who was only a few years older than me. He was telling me all about his wife's garden, and what a disaster it was, and did I have any tips for him? All around us was the buzz of voices.

"So what's with Pete?"

My ears pricked up at the mention of my name. Max was talking quietly to Damon. I did my best not to look in their direction, but strained to listen.

"What about him?" Damon's voice was low and even.

Max snorted. "Come on. You haven't brought a date to meet the family in years. The last one was Michael, and it was that long ago, you were still in college. There's probably only me and Martella who are old enough to remember him—"

"Not going there." Damon issued the words in a low growl that took me by surprise. Our eyes met once more, and I glanced away quickly, embarrassed to have been caught looking. Not so fast, however, that I didn't miss the expression on Damon's face. There had been something different about his eyes, maybe a touch less aggression than normal.

Whatever it was, I got the impression it was something I was not supposed to see.

The guests departed one by one, while I sat drinking coffee that Max provided, until there was only me, Damon, Max and their mom. Damon gestured to his watch to indicate it was time to leave.

Mrs. Ramos gave me a warm hug, which surprised the hell out of me.

"It was lovely to meet you, Pete. You make sure Damon brings you to the house for Thanksgiving, you hear?"

I peeped at Damon's face, which was turning very pink. I tried not to grin. "I'd like that." Thanksgiving was usually a quiet time for me. The idea of being around Damon's family again was a pleasant one.

Max shook my hand firmly. "Good to meet ya, Pete. Make sure you come back and eat here some time, okay? I'll sit you at the best table." He gave Damon a sideways glance before smiling at me. "You can even bring Damon."

Shit. I was trying *so* hard not to laugh.

After Damon and I had said our goodbyes, and we walked out of the restaurant's main door, I turned to him and gave him a bright smile. "That went surprisingly well."

Damon narrowed his gaze. "Too well." I was yanked by the arm into the alley where my evening had begun.

"What are you doing?"

Damon propelled me through the alley until we reached the red dumpster, where he pushed me up against the wall, out of sight of the street. My heart hammered and my throat went dry.

Damon stared at me, his eyes black. When the kiss came, it was as harsh and brutal as I'd hoped, his tongue going deep, his teeth tugging at my lips. When he reached down, popped open the button on my chinos and forced his hand into my briefs to grab my dick and squeeze it, I wanted to groan aloud with pleasure.

Except he stopped, his breathing loud and uneven.

"Just so we're clear, we are not done yet," he gritted out. "That will be after I get you to my place and in my bed."

I said the only words that made sense. "Yes, sir."

Damon's breathing hitched and his hand tightened on my cock. "Then let's find a taxi and get the fuck out of here."

He had no disagreement from me.

The taxi ride from hell.

All I wanted was to feel his hands on me but what I got was Damon keeping his distance, like there was a walrus sitting between us. I got it, sure: you never know if your cab driver might turn out to be a homophobic asshole, but still… I glanced in Damon's direction. His expression was impassive, like he hadn't just informed me we were going back to his place so he could fuck me. No emotion showing there whatsoever. Yeah, this was Damon indulging in a little mindfuckery. He was doing it on purpose.

Not that the knowledge helped alleviate my aching cock.

"Have I pissed you off in some way?" I asked. It was one reason for his silence, but I couldn't think what I'd done to warrant such a…

Wait a moment.

I got it. I fucking *got* it.

"You didn't expect that to happen, did you?" I said with a triumphant air. "You thought you'd throw me in at the deep end and I'd drown in a pool of humiliation?" That I hadn't was nothing to do with me—that was all down to Damon's family. I snorted. "Your family knows you really well, don't they? You didn't anticipate that they'd support me. Your little plan backfired."

Damon said nothing.

"I'm right, aren't I?"

Damon said nothing.

I wanted to add something, *anything*, but there

seemed little point. Damon kept his attention on his window, not once looking in my direction. I got the message. No talking. I imagined that once we got to his place, there'd be more than enough talking going on, and recalling that first time in his basement, most of it would be dirty. If part one of Damon's plan had backfired, he'd make sure part two was a damn sight more successful.

I couldn't wait.

Eventually we pulled up outside his house and by then my dick was like fucking steel. I was glad I'd worn my shirt out because that sucker was trying to peep over the waistband of my pants. Damon paid the driver and walked up to his front door, not saying a word. I followed, because hell, this was what he'd said, right? His place, his bed? I was tingling all over, aching to get fucked and anxious to know exactly how he was going to go about that task.

Once inside the house he switched on a couple of lights and went into the kitchen where he grabbed bottles of water from the refrigerator. I wasn't interested in taking a look at his place: my focus was on the two of us getting naked and me getting my ass reamed. Still nothing from him, and by then the tiniest bit of disquiet was creeping into my mind.

Is this part of it? Is Damon still fucking with my head?

Because, damn, he was good at it.

Along the hallway, through a door and there we were. Damon's bedroom. Not someplace I'd thought I'd see real soon: my interests lay in what he kept in his basement. And to tell the truth, I was kinda intrigued: what did the bedroom of a sexologist look like? As he'd led me to it, my mind was already conjuring up images of what was about to happen. I envisaged handcuffs around the bedposts, leather straps at each corner, ending in restraints, a nightstand full of sex toys, maybe hooks in the ceiling…

I wasn't prepared for the reality.

There was a bed. A very ordinary wide bed, covered in a simple blue comforter and piles of pillows. An ottoman at the foot of it, with a padded lid. A nightstand on either side of it. Two doors, both ajar, revealing his closet and his bathroom. Dark blue blinds at the windows. A tall, freestanding mirror against the wall, facing the foot of the bed. A chair next to it. And not a single sex toy or fiendish device in sight.

Okay. Okay. Now what?

Damon stopped beside the bed, facing me and…

Kissed me.

That kiss bore no resemblance to the brutal, all-teeth-and-tongues variety he'd dished up in the alley. No, *this* kiss was gentle, a brushing of lips while he caressed my cheek, his hand stroking down my arm. His tongue in my mouth, licking me, tasting me, his hand on the back of my head, holding me still while he explored me.

I froze, unsure of what he wanted from me, of where he was going with this.

Damon paused and freed my lips. Those dark eyes focused on mine. "Pete? Quit thinking so loud and kiss me."

Okay. I could kiss him.

Our lips met once more, only this time I brought my hand to the back of his head to rub over his coarse hair, cut so short it was no more than stubble. I liked that, the roughness beneath my fingertips compared to the silken touch of his lips against mine. He gave a soft noise of encouragement and I broke the kiss to move to his neck where his scent was strong, a heady, musky, male aroma. I breathed him in while I kissed the skin below his ear.

"That feels good," he said quietly.

I was so fucking lost.

I kept waiting for the pace to change, for *Damon* to change from this sensual, sexy fucker into the bear who'd fucked me in his basement. This was nothing like the Damon I knew.

What if this is the real Damon? It really messed with my head.

But still, I had to admit, what he was doing felt really... good.

When he gently pushed me off, my heartbeat sped up. *Okay. Okay. This is it.*

"Go stand at the foot of the bed and take off your jacket."

I did as instructed, Damon beside me while he removed his own. He took mine and placed them both over the chair. "Stand in front of the mirror."

I stared at my reflection, the flush on my chest beneath the shirt, my bright eyes, the line of my dick visible, my chinos pulled taut over my erection. Damon moved to stand behind me, heat radiating from him. He reached around under my arms and slowly began to unbutton my shirt, his gaze focused on the mirror. I found myself watching his progress as he moved lower, until he got to the waistband of my chinos. I bit my lip as he rubbed over my crotch, his fingers tracing the line of my cock.

When he popped open the button and slid the zipper down, my heart pounded, and my dick twitched in anticipation.

Damon pushed my chinos past my hips so that they fell to the floor, but he made no move to take them off. Instead, he languidly rubbed his hand over my crotch, where my dick was already making a wet spot on my briefs. When he resumed unbuttoning my shirt, ignoring my aching shaft, I want to growl, to tell him to get his goddamn hand back where I wanted it. My frustration was short-lived when he pulled open the flaps of my shirt and rubbed my cock through my briefs, until it pushed obscenely at the fabric.

Damon removed my shirt and placed it on the chair with the jackets.

I clenched my hands into fists at my sides. I wanted more, but I knew better. This was Damon's show, Damon's payback for me fucking him.

The bastard was trying to drive me crazy.

He had one hand on my belly, rubbing it, while the other stroked up and down my shaft, the movement leisurely, like he had all the time in the world. When he moved higher to tweak my nipple, I pushed out a low groan. Damon chuckled and slid his hand inside my briefs to wrap his fingers around my cock.

Fuck, that felt amazing, his hands on me, arousing me while I watched him do it, saw my flushed face, my parted lips, the glazed expression in my eyes. Damon kissed my shoulder and pulled his hand free of my briefs.

No, I wanted to yell. *Don't stop.*

"Eyes on the mirror," he said, his voice quiet. "Watch."

I held my breath as he knelt behind me, grasped the waistband of my briefs and slowly, so slowly, lowered them over my erect dick that sprang up, slapping against my belly with a dull thud. He paused, my briefs around my knees, and I gasped when he kissed my ass, biting gently, before...

"What do we have here?" He sounded amused. I gasped again when he pulled gently on the butt plug.

"Well, what did you expect?" I retorted. "I was meeting *you*! I had to be prepared for any eventuality, right?"

Laughing, Damon pulled the plug slowly from my hole. "I always appreciate initiative." He spread me with both hands and pushed his face into my crack, rubbing his nose and beard over my hole before briefly licking it. I trembled, my legs shaking from the effort of holding myself upright while he pushed his tongue inside me. But all too soon, he'd finished, and I wanted to groan with frustration.

Damon rose to his feet and stood in front of me. By now my briefs and chinos were around my ankles and I couldn't move. Damon proceeded to stroke my shaft and balls, pausing to rub his thumb over the slit and draw out the pre-cum like a thread of shining silk.

I knew there would be a lot more of that before we were done. Then all such thoughts fled when he bent lower to take my cock in his mouth.

"Oh fuck."

Damon chuckled around my dick and knelt in front of me, one hand cupping my balls while he sucked the head of my cock, now and again sliding those full lips down the shaft but never taking it deep enough to satisfy me. His other hand was on my ass, squeezing it, holding me steady while he went down on me. I thrust gently into that glorious mouth, but he just moved his head back, controlling the depth.

When he stopped, I wanted to curse his teasing black soul.

Damon began to unbutton his own shirt. "Shoes off. Step out of your briefs and pants," he ordered, "and place them on the chair."

I toed off my shoes and hurriedly shucked off my pants and underwear. I scooped them up off the floor, shaking them out and putting them on the chair. When I turned back to Damon, I caught my breath at the sight of that barrel chest, covered in a silky mat of hair, his nipples erect. It never failed: one look at that solid, furry chest and torso was enough to have more pre-cum leaking from my slit.

Damon removed his belt and unfastened his pants. When he dropped them to reveal a pair of black boxers, his erection very obvious, I swear, I started drooling. Damon grinned as he pushed them off, his dick thick and hard, curving upward. He removed his shoes and stepped out of his clothes while I stood there, wearing only a pair of white ankle socks.

Damon straightened and slipped his hands around me to cup my asscheeks, squeezing them while he slowly ground his cock against mine. I groaned as his mouth took mine again, tongue pushing deep while his fingers caressed my ass, edging closer to my crack.

Fuck, yeah. Touch my hole.

Only, he didn't.

Damon lifted me, surprising me with his strength, and gently lowered me onto the bed. "Scoot up the bed, your head on the pillows."

I moved swiftly, legs falling apart, my gaze fixed on him. He pulled off my socks and then, thank fuck, there he was between my legs, kissing me, his body a warm, solid weight on mine. I arched as he shifted lower to tease my nipples with his teeth, hands stroking my chest, his cock sliding over mine, hot, silken skin covering a rod of rigid flesh.

I went to touch him, to stroke his back, but he grasped my wrists and placed my hands above my head. His eyes met mine briefly, and the message was clear enough: *Keep them there.* Then he stroked my biceps, moving lower to rub my chest while he kissed a path down to my dick.

Fuck. Oh fuck, yes.

Damon paused, his lips inches from the head of my cock, already wet with pre-cum. I couldn't take my eyes off him. I held my breath, willing him to just fucking *do* it, to take me so deep that I would feel his throat tight around me, his nose buried in my pubes.

What he did was to lap up the pre-cum, before tracing a line down my shaft, taking his time, his gaze fixed on my face. I couldn't breathe, couldn't move, mesmerized by the sight of that agile tongue as he licked up and down my length, flicking the ridge under the head before teasing that sweet spot under it, until I was writhing, pushing my cock against his lips, wanting more.

When his hot mouth encased my dick, I pushed my head back into the pillows and sighed with pleasure. I pushed up with my hips, the only thought in my head to fuck his mouth.

Damon had other plans. He pulled free of my cock and crawled up my body to kiss me, wrapping a large hand around both our lengths. I moaned into his kiss, rocking against him, my pre-cum making everything slick. When both of us were moaning softly, he grabbed onto me and rolled us until I was on top, my leg astride him.

Then the kissing started again, only this time we rocked against each other, Damon reaching between our bodies to rub our cocks together. I forgot about payback, mindfucking, *everything* except for the way he was making me feel. I shifted my weight onto my arms and propped myself up while he kissed my chest and neck, his fingers sliding into my crease. When I bowed my head to meet his gaze, Damon's eyes locked on me and *fuck*, the look in them was so hot, my heart quaked. His hands didn't stop touching me, caressing me, and I couldn't stop kissing him. I wrapped my hand around his shaft and tugged, while he cupped my ass and rocked me against his body.

When he reached around to spread my ass, a single finger tapping against my hole, I arched my back and shifted higher up his body to give him greater access.

"You want my cock in there, don't you?" he murmured against my chest.

I groaned aloud. "Like you have to ask." My body ached to feel him inside me.

Damon chuckled. "Good to know we both want the same thing." He flicked his head toward the nightstand. "Top drawer. Lube and condoms."

I knelt up, leaned across and yanked it open, feeling with my fingertips. When I met the smooth surface of the bottle and the foil packets, I grinned. "Bingo." I grabbed them and dropped them onto the bed beside us.

Damon picked up a condom and tore open the packet. "Gonna do this now," he said as he unrolled the latex down his heavy, wide shaft. "Don't want to delay us when I'm ready to fuck you." When that was done, he snapped open the bottle and slicked up his fingers. He finished lubing up his cock and met my gaze. "I want to watch you fuck yourself with your fingers." His gaze locked on mine. "Kiss me while you do it."

Fuck. Heat flooded my body at the thought of his hard dick inside me, and my hole clenched tight. I straddled him, and then his mouth was on mine, neither of us quiet this time. The room was filled with the sound of our breathing, harsh and loud, as we kissed and rocked, kissed and rocked, my desire and need spiraling ever higher. I reached back to press two fingers into my hole, pushing back onto it as soon as it felt comfortable. Damon stroked my chest and the back of my head, his tongue battling with mine, his own noises of desire increasing in volume. By the time I was sliding my fingers easily, both of us emitted soft gasps and low cries, both plainly eager for what was coming.

I pulled free of my body to grasp his slippery dick, and shifted until the head of his cock pressed against my hole.

"Do it," Damon urged, his breathing heavy.

I sat back, slowly lowering my body onto his shaft, until he was all the way inside me. My dick jerked up toward my belly and Damon collected pre-cum on his fingers, bringing them to his lips to taste me. I held myself still, while Damon stroked my thighs, my hips, my belly, before tilting his hips and pulling me down into a kiss. Little hums of satisfaction emanated from both of us when he began to push into me, hips rocking, our lips fused into kiss after kiss. His hands were on my ass, spreading my cheeks while he slid into my hole. I groaned into his mouth and grabbed the headboard to steady myself as he filled my channel, his wide cock stretching me.

Fuck, I'd missed this. There had been no one inside me since our last fuck. The last three weeks had comprised of me fucking myself with a dildo, the memory of our hot coupling playing over and over in my head on a loop.

The real thing was infinitely better.

Damon grabbed onto me and flipped us so that I ended up on my back.

"Wait," I called out breathlessly, and before he could thrust into me, I lifted my legs to rest on his shoulders and began to roll my hips up off the bed, fucking myself on his dick. Damon groaned and propped himself up on his hands, letting me control it. I pushed up with my hips, my movements gaining in momentum…

Until he stopped me with a kiss, his tongue going deep.

I could not get enough of Damon's mouth on mine.

Slowly, deliberately, Damon rotated his hips, his face hovering above mine, our eyes focused on each other. I shifted my legs to wrap them around him, and he stretched out on top of me, still continuing with that slow press of his cock into my hole, that leisurely circling of his hips that had nerve endings firing up all over my body. He buried his face in my neck and kissed me there, before kneeling up to stroke my dick. I placed my foot against his chest and rubbed over his nipple with my toes, making him moan softly. When he eased his cock out of me, I groaned.

Gently, Damon rolled me onto my belly, before lifting my hips until I was on all fours, knees tucked under me.

"Okay, now fuck yourself on my cock," he instructed, his voice husky.

I pushed back, loving the way our soft moans mingled to produce one erotic soundtrack. I rocked onto that thick dick, moving faster, until he slowed me with both hands flat to my ass. Then he used his body to push me onto the mattress, my cock trapped against it. His hands covered mine as he continued to rock into me, hips rolling fluidly while he kissed the back of my neck, my shoulders, between my shoulder blades, his knees pushing mine wider. When he lifted my chin to kiss my mouth, I pushed a low moan between his lips.

This was beyond anything I had ever experienced. Damon was playing me like an instrument, and fuck, my whole body was *singing* for him. I didn't want it to come to an end. That slow circling of his hips, stirring his cock inside me, was driving me out of my mind. When he paused to pull out of me and place a line of soft, languid kisses up my spine, I wanted to cry out, to tell him to finish me because it was too good, too sensual...

I was lost for adjectives.

Then he was rolling me onto my back, pushing my knees toward my chest, his own chest heaving. His gaze traveled up my body to my face, and when our eyes met, I shivered, not knowing why I did it.

Damon grabbed hold of my ankles and sank his dick deep inside me, pushing the air from my lungs. He fucked me with long strokes until I was breathless with need.

"Please... Damon, please."

Fuck. His pupils were blown, his eyes almost black.

My legs rested once more on his shoulders, his

face inches from mine, his breath hot on my lips. "Touch yourself," he growled.

I grabbed my dick and tugged, my balls tight against my body. I was so close, my climax imminent. Damon kept his thrusts short, his gaze locked on mine.

He wants me to cum first.

I tugged harder, my cock slick with lube and pre-cum, my breathing growing more erratic as I neared orgasm. When I shot hard, cum exploding from my dick to hit my chin and chest. Damon groaned loudly. "Fuck, yeah. Fucking beautiful." He stilled inside me while I shuddered, body jolted by mini shocks, overwhelmed by an orgasm that had taken my breath away.

When I'd eased down from my high, Damon began to fuck me with long, deep strokes, so forceful that soon my head was banging against the headboard with each thrust, his hips jerking as he buried his cock deep inside me. He picked up speed, fucking me until I was crying out with every thrust, desperate to feel his dick throb in me.

When his orgasm hit, I felt it through me, felt his cock swell inside my channel, his body tremble against mine. Damon fused our mouths in a lingering kiss, his hands on my chest, my face, my neck, his touch gentle. I cupped his nape and returned his kiss, sighing into his mouth when he rotated his hips once again, his dick still inside me.

When Damon finally became still, I put my arms around him. "That was amazing," I sighed.

Damon caressed my cheek and smiled. "And not what you were expecting?"

I laughed, and his softened cock slipped from my body. Damon grabbed hold of the condom and removed it carefully. Once he'd dropped it into the trash can beside the bed, he settled back on top of me, his body between my legs.

"That was *so* not what I was expecting," I confessed. My body was warm and sated, and there was a delicious ache that I knew would remain with me for a while.

Damon nodded. "I like to keep you on your toes," he said, his eyes sparkling.

It was only then that the thought occurred to me. At some point in the... proceedings, I'd stopped waiting for Damon to revert to the man who'd had me fastened to his St. Andrew's Cross, and I'd simply let myself enjoy what was happening. And yes, it had not been what I expected—in some strange way it had been better. Hotter.

"Put it this way. After that performance, I have no idea what's coming next." Then it struck me I was being presumptive. "That is, *if* anything is coming next," I added hastily.

Damon snickered. "Funny you should say that." He rolled off me and lay on the bed next to me. "What are you doing in two weeks' time? The weekend of September 26?"

I did a quick mental calculation. "I think I'm free, as far as I can remember. Why?"

"There's somewhere I'd like to take you." He cocked his head to one side. "Have you ever been to the Folsom Street Fair?"

Just the words were enough to make my gut roll over. "No," I said, drawing out the syllable, "but I've always wanted to. I've never had the nerve, I suppose." Plus there was no way I'd go there on my own.

Damon beamed. "That settles it. You're

coming with me." His gaze narrowed. "Except there's something we'll have to take care of before we can go."

"Oh?" For some reason my stomach churned.

He nodded. "You and I are gonna pay a visit to Mr. S. I'm not gonna have my boy look out of place."

Mr. S? I knew the name, of course. Mr. S Leather. *The* place for all things leather in San Francisco. Not to mention a variety of toys and implements for the kinky at heart.

Then it hit me. What I'd almost missed.

"Your… your boy?" My chest tightened.

Damon nodded once more, his smile fading. "That is, if you're still interested."

Gone was the Damon I'd known so far. *This* Damon was deadly serious.

This matters to him. This is important.

When realization came, it struck with such force that I was left dumbfounded.

Yes, I was interested. And yes, it mattered to me too.

I said the only words that would do, given the circumstances.

"Yes, sir."

LIMITS

TANTALUS

LIMITS

Pete finally gets to go to the Folsom Street Fair.
It's a weekend for exploring his limits.
But ultimately it's Damon's limits that are challenged.

Limits

A Shopping Trip

Pete

I was a kid in a candy store. Only thing was, I didn't know where to start.

I made straight for the leather shorts, kilts and pants, and fuck, the *smell* of them was enough to make my dick hard. Then there were the outfits in rubber, not really my thing but it takes all sorts, right?

The collars, ball-gags, tawses, floggers and whips. *Holy fuck.*

Then there was the wall—an entire *wall*—full of dildos that could have been Emmy awards, they were so pretty. Not to mention fucking *huge*. Bronze, black, you name it, Mr. S Leather provided it. Some of them made my eyes water, just thinking about something that size getting anywhere *near* my hole, let alone in it.

What really caught my attention was the glass cabinet in the center of the store.

Cock rings, a mouth-watering selection. Wicked-looking sounds in all sizes and materials. And fiendish implements that made me want to wince and drool, all at the same time. Spikes, designed to deliver exquisite torture to some lucky boy's cock and balls.

It was a kink lover's paradise, and Damon had turned me loose in it.

Not that *I* fit into that category, you understand. I was merely a *wannabe* kink lover. I stood by the rack of leather shorts, my gaze glued to the widescreen TV suspended from the ceiling, which was showing a hardcore BDSM scene featuring a couple of porn actors that I recognized instantly.

How many guys watch this and fight the urge to jerk off in the store? My palm was itching to wrap itself around my dick.

A throat cleared. "When you're done salivating..."

Damon stood behind me, watching me, a big shit-grin all over his face.

Oops.

I gave a sheepish shrug. "Well, what did you expect when you brought me here?"

Damon arched his eyebrows. "Down, boy. We're here on a mission. We need to find you something to wear for tomorrow." His grin widened. "And I know just where to begin." He crooked his finger, beckoning me to follow him to a stand full of... shorts and jocks.

Holy Fucking Hell, they left nothing to the imagination. I stared at the *really* short shorts, that looked like they would fit extremely tightly across my crotch. Damon pulled out one pair and handed them to me. "Hold onto those. You're gonna try them on in a moment."

The leather was black, shiny and God, it was thin. "Damon, if I wear these, anyone who gets within several feet of me is going to know I'm cut."

There was that grin again. "That's the general idea." He returned his attention to the rack. "Now what we need is a leather jock. Something with easy access, but nice and tight to show off that gorgeous cock." He riffled through the garments, before pulling one from the array with a triumphant noise. "There. Perfect. Those buttons on the front and that zip mean you'll be able to get your dick out at a moment's notice. It also means I get quick access to your shaft. I call that a win-win situation." He thrust the item into my hand.

I gazed at the skimpy garments, and it was only then that the thought came to mind. "Er... where am I going to be wearing these?"

Damon folded his arms across his wide chest. "The shorts are for tomorrow, when we're visiting the street fair."

"And what will I be wearing with them?" I had a sneaking feeling I wasn't going to like the answer.

"Boots."

"Boots," I repeated heavily. "That... that's it?"

Damon laughed. "Of course not."

I heaved an internal sigh of relief.

"You'll have a collar on, and I'll attach a leash to that."

Oh. My. God. He was going to make me walk through the streets of San Francisco in nothing but boots, a jock and a collar. "You don't think I'll attract a bit of attention in that outfit?" I had to admit, the prospect was both scary as shit... and sexy as fuck.

Damon snorted. "You and the rest of the

submissives. If you're that bashful, you can cover up, dainty boy, until we get there. Then you get to strip and show off that gorgeous bod." He pointed toward the changing area, a couple of cubicles that were separated from the store by green curtains. "Try on the shorts first, then get your ass out here. I want to see how they look on you."

"You and everyone else in the store," I muttered as I walked toward the one empty cubicle. Of course, if Damon was going to have me marching down Folsom Street in this getup, maybe I'd better get used to the idea pretty damn quick.

I pulled the curtain, kicked off my shoes and squirmed out of my jeans. My first thought was that I'd need talcum powder to get my ass anywhere *near* the shorts. I held them open, stepped into them and tugged them up. One glance in the mirror sent a thrill of anticipation humming through me.

"Fuck, you can see every vein in my dick," I muttered.

"Sounds good to me." Damon's voice right on the other side of the curtain made me jump. "Now get out here so I can see for myself."

My heartbeat still racing, I stepped beyond the green curtain to where Damon awaited me, still grinning, the bastard. His gaze flickered down to my crotch and he nodded slowly. "Very nice. Very nice indeed." He moved closer and grabbed my ass, squeezing the cheek hard, his other hand palming my full erection that the shorts merely served to exaggerate. "Have I ever told you what a gorgeous cock you have?"

"You might have mentioned it," I said breathlessly, pushing into his touch.

Of course, the teasing black-hearted bastard

Damon & Pete: Playing with Fire

took his hand away at that point.

He swatted me on the butt. "Okay, now show me the jock." He propelled me toward the changing booth again, his hand to my back.

Getting out of a pair of skin-tight leather shorts is a good deal more difficult than getting into them.

The jock just about held my dick captive, the leather snug against my skin, the zipper biting into my shaft a little where it strained to be released. I tried to peer over my shoulder to see what my ass looked like. *Damn, they need two mirrors in here.*

I pulled back the curtain to find Damon in conversation with another guy, seemingly discussing the camo leather shorts the stranger was trying on. The guy had his back turned to me, but even so, there was something familiar about him. He was about five feet nine, a solid mass of muscle, broad across the back, his biceps thick. Before I could say a word, Damon's gaze met mine.

"Eyes to the floor, Pete, arms by your sides. And stay like that until I tell you otherwise."

What the fuck? I'd have thought it a joke, except I knew that tone of voice by now. Quickly I lowered my gaze.

"Just here to get some trappings for tomorrow." This was obviously meant for the stranger.

"You're going to the street fair? Awesome! You'll have to come by and say hi. I'll be working the Mr. S booth." There was a pause. "They look like a really nice, tight fit."

"Turn around," Damon instructed me.

His firm tone sent a shiver straight to my balls. Fuck. I was getting to love it when he talked to me like that. I held myself still, pulse racing.

"Fuck, that's a gorgeous ass," the guy said, his deep resonant voice reminding me a little of Damon. "May I?"

Damon chuckled. "Be my guest."

I held my breath to keep from gasping when the guy stroked a warm hand over my ass. "Have you ever marked him?"

"Only with my hand, but it's definitely on my list." Another hand, this one Damon's, gently squeezing me.

I stood there in the middle of the store while two men fondled my ass, discussing marking me with... God knows what. Not something I'd ever seen coming—well, only in my fantasies.

Then it was over, and they released me.

"You can turn around now," Damon told me.

I faced them, my dick harder than ever. All it took was Damon clearing his throat to have me remembering where I was supposed to be looking. The guy spoke up. "Ooh. And that's even nicer. You're a lucky man, Damon."

I was listening. That brief glimpse of the guy had fired up something in my brain. And that voice. I *knew* that voice.

"Thanks. But you're right about those shorts. They need some sort of a pouch built in."

"Tell me about it," the guy groaned. "It's way too tight across my dick. And speaking of which, I'd better get out of them. Don't forget to come say hi tomorrow."

Damon answered for me. "We will."

The guy stepped back into the other changing booth. I was doing a really bad job of trying not to appear like I was peeking.

"The jock looks good."

With a start I realized Damon was talking to me. "Oh. Yeah. Okay."

He chuckled. "Get dressed. I'll be over there when you're done." He pointed toward... that center glass cabinet. The one with all the fiendish devices.

My heart skipped a beat. *Is he going to ...?*

"Pete. Clothes. Now."

Yeah. Okay. Don't think about it.

"Pete."

I knew that tone. I hurried into the booth and removed the jock. When I was dressed, I exited the booth. The next door one was empty and there was no sign of its occupant. I walked over to Damon, who was peering at a display of cock rings and butt plugs. He straightened as I approached, the two items in my hand.

He took them from me. "I'll just get these, and then we're out of here."

It was then that I noticed the black plastic bag at his feet.

Damon's been shopping. And whatever he's bought, he's not telling.

My balls tingled and my palms grew clammy.

I followed him to the cash desk, waiting to one side while he paid. I glanced around, noting all the huge photos displayed at ceiling height, showing gorgeous men in Mr. S gear. One such photo sent a shockwave rippling through me.

"Holy fuck." *Now* I remembered where I'd heard that voice before.

"Anything wrong?"

I spun around to stare at Damon, who was still wearing that perpetual grin of his.

"You might have told me." I knew it came out as a whine, but *Jesus*...

Damon opened his eyes wide. "I have no idea what you're talking about."

Yeah, right.

I pointed to the graphic. "That was him, wasn't it? In the changing booth?"

"Possibly."

The bastard. Of course he'd known.

I took a calming breath. "I was talking to *Dirk Caber* and you said nothing? Do you have any idea how many of his films are on my hard drive? I've been jerking off to him for the last four years, for Christ's sake." Then it hit me. "Oh my fucking God—Dirk Caber grabbed my ass." One of the hottest porn stars I'd ever seen had fondled my ass. Hell, he'd admired my dick.

"Don't tell me—you didn't recognize him with his clothes on. Didn't I tell you?" Damon smiled. "He's a friend of mine."

Some recollections clicked into place. BDSM videos, shot right here in San Francisco. Dirk asking for permission before he squeezed my ass. Asking if Damon had marked me yet. "Oh God," I moaned. "He's another Dom, isn't he?"

Damon nodded. "And a damn good one." He leaned closer. "You did me proud, boy."

Wow. It was amazing how *fucking good* those four words made me feel. "I did?" A surge of warmth spread throughout my body, and I stood up straight.

Damon chuckled. "And that's enough ego stroking for now. I'm taking you home, and after we've had dinner, you and I are going to have a little chat."

"Oh? What about?"

My skin prickled when his gaze met mine. "There are a few things we have to get straight before tomorrow."

I couldn't help it. I snorted. "Hate to tell you this, but neither of us is straight."

He smacked my ass, right there in front of the guy behind the cash desk.

"Hey, that hurt!"

Damon guffawed. "Boy, you've had worse from me, so don't give me that shit." His eyes narrowed. "Yeah, we need to make sure your head's in the right space for tomorrow."

The urge to laugh ebbed away, and there was that tingling all over my arms and back again. Whatever he was going to talk about was obviously serious.

I sobered. "Yes, Sir." I was a fast learner. If I wanted to please him, I called him Sir.

He grunted and thrust the plastic bag containing my new shorts and jock into my hands. "Now get that pretty ass out of here."

That grunt was typical Damon, but the slow smile was something new.

I liked that I'd put it there.

Damon

I loaded the dishwasher before taking a last glance around the kitchen. Every surface was devoid of clutter, just how I liked it.

"You can learn a lot about a man from looking at the way he lives." Pete stood in the doorway, arms folded.

I arched my eyebrows. "Is that so? And what does my house tell you about me?"

"That you like everything just so. Neat. Tidy. You like order."

I snorted. "I'm a fucking Dom. That much you could have worked out without ever stepping across my threshold."

He nodded. "Sure, but what I see confirms what I already know."

I handed him a mug of coffee and gave him a hard stare. "I thought I told you to go sit on the couch and wait for me."

Pete bit his lip. "Are you always this bossy, even when you're not fucking me?"

I pointed. "Living room. Now. Before I decide to pull down those tight jeans and take my paddle to your ass."

He walked away from me, snickering.

Yeah, the little shit would probably enjoy that. I was starting to get the measure of him. There were an awful lot of holes, however. Tonight was going to be a kind of 'fill in the blanks' session.

I followed him into the living room and nodded in approval to find him sitting as instructed, his hands wrapped around the mug. I sat beside him and leaned back.

"How old are you?"

Pete blinked and laughed.

"What's so funny about that?"

He gave a casual shrug. "It seems a funny question, given the circumstances." When I said nothing but stared at him, he smiled. "You know how to make me scream when we fuck, how to push my buttons, but when it comes down to it, you don't know a whole lot about me, do you?" His eyes sparkled. "I guess it's a matter of 'need to know.' You don't need to know all that shit when all we do is fuck."

Except we were past that, after I'd taken him to Mama's birthday meal.

Before I could come back with a sharp retort, he relaxed into the couch. "I'm twenty-eight."

I recalled what I'd overheard at the party. "You're an only child and your parents are dead." He nodded. "Did you grow up here in San Francisco?"

"No, in Florida. I studied here though. When my parents died, I moved here."

"You left Florida for San Francisco? Boy, do you like the cold or something?"

Pete laughed. "I like it here, all right? Besides, there was nothing to keep me in Florida, only memories." His face tightened.

Okay, maybe he wasn't as crazy as I'd thought. He sat stiffer than before, his expression neutral.

I changed the subject, determined to raise a smile. "So, have you always been a kinky little shit?"

Christ, he nearly spluttered coffee all over the couch.

"Did I touch a nerve?"

Pete flushed. It was such an unexpected reaction, and fucking adorable. "When I was a kid, I used to collect action figures. Nothing unusual about that, except that... Spiderman used to tie up Batman."

I chuckled. "There you go. Why am I not surprised?" It provided me with a nice segue, however. "That's actually what I wanted us to discuss before tomorrow."

I was pleased to note how he straightened, his focus sharpening. "Okay."

"You remember I asked if you wanted to be my boy." It had been two weeks ago, but I could still recall the look on his face. Sort of an 'Oh my God it's Christmas come early' expression.

"Yes, Sir." His voice was softer.

I shifted on the couch to face him. "Well, there are some things we have to work out before I take you to the fair."

"Like what?"

"Limits." I cocked my head. "Do you know what I'm talking about?" It was fine if he didn't. That was the purpose of the conversation, after all.

"You mean, you want to know what stuff I'd have no problems with, and the stuff I wouldn't ever consider doing in a month of Sundays."

It was my turn to laugh. "Yeah, but you might be surprised to learn that the stuff you say *No way José* to now, might not stay that way." I took a sip of coffee before continuing. "For instance, I may not know you all that well, but I know enough to be fairly confident that bondage is going to be something you have no qualms about. Spiderman and Batman were a bit of a giveaway."

He chuckled. "Yeah, I suppose."

"But what might be a soft limit for you is where and when that takes place."

"Soft limit?" He scrunched up his eyebrows.

"A soft limit means you're happy to do it, but you might hesitate about it or place certain conditions on it in specific circumstances."

"Wow." He stared at me, eyes wide.

"What?"

Pete smiled. "We're really going to do this."

I guess the penny had finally dropped. I nodded. "Yes, we are." I pulled my phone from my pocket and scrolled through, searching for a file.

"You know, you don't sound the same as you did, that first time in your basement."

I glanced up to find him regarding me thoughtfully. "Oh?"

Pete nodded slowly. "Back then you were gruffer, coarser."

"And exactly like you'd expected me to sound."

His eyes widened. "How... how did you know that?"

I chuckled. "Once you'd seen how my basement was kitted out, you thought I'd be like the guys you'd seen on the internet. How you imagined a Dom to be." Not that I'd known that right away. That realization had come as I'd gotten to know him a little better. That first night, though, I'd played a role, and he'd lapped it up.

My dick stiffened at the memory of Pete on all fours, lapping up cum from the floor because I'd told him to. That act alone had told me the boy had potential.

"Maybe," he admitted. "But what about now?"

"Now we need to be honest with each other, to be ourselves. I don't expect you to hide what you want from me, or else what would be the point? And you need to see me as I am, to know I will take care of your needs." *And you.* Shit. *Danger, Will Robinson, danger.* Maybe I should file that little afterthought far away for now.

He gazed at me in silence for a moment before nodding again. "That make sense."

I snickered. "Glad to hear it." I handed Pete the phone. "This is a basic list. I need you to tell me what would be fine and dandy as far as you're concerned, what you might possibly think about doing if not right now, and what would be a hard limit for you." I grinned. "That would be your 'Hell No' list." I already had a fair idea of where he'd draw the line, but I'd been surprised before.

Pete perused the list and drew in a sharp breath. "I think I've just found my first hard limit."

I waited, sipping my coffee.

He grimaced. "Scat."

Yeah, like I hadn't seen that one coming. "Okay. Good to know. What about water sports?" It wasn't something I was all that keen on, but I'd need to know if he was.

"Possibly?" The word crept out of him, his hesitation so fucking cute.

"Duly noted."

My reaction seemed to relax him. He breathed more easily and focused on the list. "So yeah, my 'absolutely gotta have these' are bondage, spanking and toys."

I snorted. "Tell me something I didn't know." When he nodded absently, his teeth worrying his lip, my curiosity was aroused. "Okay, I'll bite. What's got you so thoughtful?"

He raised his chin. "Exhibitionism, for one thing."

I couldn't resist. "Seeing as I'm going to be parading you along Folsom Street in a pair of ridiculously tight leather shorts tomorrow, I'd say that was a good thing." He laughed, and I went in for the kill. "Of course, that would also cover me spanking you in public. Fucking you." I gazed at him, not breaking eye contact. "That still okay?"

The sharp intake of breath and the way his eyes glazed over was answer enough. I grinned to myself. It looked like my plans for the following day were still in the cards.

Time to push him a bit farther.

"What about others?" I kept my tone even.

"Others?" He knitted his brows. "What do you mean?"

"What if I decide to involve other people in what we do?"

He swallowed. Hard. "What would that entail, exactly?"

I gave a shrug. "Letting them touch you. Kiss you." I locked gazes with him. "Fuck you. With me present, of course."

Fuck, his eyes were huge. "I... I think that might be one of those soft limits you mentioned." His voice cracked slightly.

I cocked my head to one side. "So it's not an outright no, it's a 'let's see how I feel should the occasion arise'?"

He gave another careful nod. "Yes."

It was more than I'd expected. It would be interesting to see how he reacted when the time came. Because now I fully intended for the occasion to present itself.

"You said, for one thing. Is there something else?"

He nodded. "Fisting," he said quietly, more subdued now. I guess I'd given him something to think about.

It was then that I recalled that first time in my

basement. I'd mentioned fisting him then, and his reaction had been interesting. He'd frozen, but not before I'd seen something in his eyes, his face, something that had made me think Pete wouldn't always be averse to having my hand inside his ass.

"That will be something for us to work toward," I said, still keeping my voice low and even. "We're talking a whole lot of trust between us before we go down that road."

Pete nodded. "I'm okay with that." He spoke calmly, and I was so fucking proud of him for speaking up.

This was going to be interesting.

When it became apparent that he was fine with the rest of the list, I made a decision.

"I want you to go back to your place tonight."

Christ, he looked like a little puppy that had been kicked, and the sight tugged at my insides. "I... I can't stay with you tonight?"

I shook my head. "I want you to spend some time alone and think about what we've discussed." I softened the blow. "But tomorrow night? I'm taking you some place special."

His eyes widened. "Where?"

"A party hosted by some friends of mine. They have an apartment overlooking Folsom Street." I'd saved the best for last. "It's a sex party. Ever been to one of those?"

Fuck, his eyes were huge. "No." In that instant I knew what he was thinking, not that it was all that difficult: *Sex party* went hand in hand with *others*, after all.

"Then this will be quite an experience." I had plans for that tight ass. "And afterward, you can come back here and stay the night." I was going to want him close, especially if the party went as I intended.

Pete was going to be my boy, lock stock and barrel.

All the fun of the fair

Pete

I had never felt so naked in my life.

I was grateful for the day's temperature: at least I wasn't freezing my ass off. I kept reaching up to touch the collar Damon had placed around my neck before we'd left his place. The way he'd looked at me when he fastened it… It was enough to make me thrust my chest out and hold my chin high. A leather leash was clipped to the D ring at the front, Damon holding the other end. A slow nod of approval made me feel ten feet tall, but better still was the kiss that followed. It was as if he claimed my mouth as his.

"Is it what you expected?"

I snorted. "God, no."

I'd expected leather, a sea of it. I'd expected to see lots of harnesses fitted snugly across broad, furry chests. Chaps and leather pants, encasing bulging thigh muscles and prominently displaying full, heavy dicks. An ocean of men, and the scent and taste of testosterone in the air.

But… pushchairs? Mothers with *pushchairs*?

I'd read up on the street fair, its early days, the kind of guys who'd frequented it. Never having gotten up sufficient nerve to see for myself, I made do with staring at lots and lots of photos. But the reality was far different.

The street was packed, but not the way I'd anticipated. Sure, the fair was loud, music playing from several different points along the way, and everywhere I looked, something was going on, but still, the whole scene left me with the impression that somehow Folsom had been... diluted.

"Tell me what you're thinking," Damon pushed.

"It's not a case of what I expected to see, more a case of what I didn't."

He followed my gaze with his own. "Yeah, there's a lot of sports kit, isn't there?"

There was, to the point where it seemed there was more casual wear than leather. Guys walked around in long shorts with their asses hanging out.

"It's not just that," I remonstrated. "It's the sheer diversity of body types." Yes, there were the lean, muscled, fit men I'd expected, but there were also the woefully unfit. I lowered my voice and leaned in closer. "I'm finding it so ironic that the men who should be showing off a lot of skin aren't, whereas those men who, God help them, really *shouldn't* have that much acreage of flesh on display, are the ones walking around in next-to-nothing—or in some cases, nothing." Then I had second thoughts. Surely it was a good thing that they felt comfortable enough to be themselves? My chest tightened and I swallowed. Body shaming was for assholes.

Damon chuckled. "I hope you're not including me in that last statement."

I snorted. "As if. You're fucking gorgeous and you know it." Then I snapped my mouth shut. I hadn't intended to be that honest.

Damon's arm slipped around my waist and he kissed my cheek, a surprisingly tender gesture. "Nice to know my efforts are appreciated." He straightened. "I'd be the first to admit that Folsom has changed in recent years. There was this one guy who came every year. His thing was to lie naked in the middle of the sidewalk and jack off. When he was done, he'd get up, move to someplace else and do it all over again. Last year? There he was, doing his thing, but surrounded by a group of giggling Japanese girls, all dressed in pink, pointing at him and taking pictures. I remember thinking at the time, *I can see it now when they get home and show their folks their holiday photos. 'This is what Americans do.'*" He shook his head. "Folsom is becoming a tourist spectacle."

There was certainly plenty for tourists to look at. Leather gear, rubber, guys crawling on all fours in puppy masks, complete with puppy tail butt plugs, guys strolling around with their dicks poking out of their shorts... There were even a few Furries.

"And if you think it's busy now," Damon said, gesturing to the street, "you should see it after three o'clock. Then it gets *really* jammed."

So far, I'd seen lots of stalls. There were any amount of vendors, selling leather gear, rubber, you name it, but there were also stalls for community groups, the gay rugby team, and a stall where you could get tested for HIV. As we progressed along Folsom Street, we passed the Kink.com booth, where they'd set up a dungeon scenario, but I got the sense that it wasn't typical BDSM but rather a watered down version. When I said as much to Damon, he nodded in agreement.

"This is more for spectacle." He pointed to a couple of guys on the stage. "Those two are porn stars, as are all of the guys performing here. Their background is more modeling than BDSM. Watch."

I watched as one guy bent another over a bench and smacked his ass.

"See? You won't see floggers or whips here, or even paddles. Their hands make a good loud noise, and that's what they're after. And look at their facial expressions. They're trying to *look* like they're being mean, when actually... "

I nodded too. We reached the Mr. S stall that had been set up next to a stage, complete with padded bench, a St. Andrew's cross and a bondage table with little hooks all the way around it. Men of all shapes and sizes were packed in around it, watching.

"Hey, there's your new admirer," Damon said, nudging my arm and grinning.

On the stage, Dirk Caber was tying up a member of the audience with black ropes, keeping up a running commentary. I couldn't catch the words, but people were laughing. I had to admit, he clearly knew what he was doing.

"They'll do demos in flogging and bondage all day," Damon told me.

Across the street was another demo, this time of puppy handling, involving one large guy and three men in puppy gear. The street was more tightly packed at that point, and Damon stopped me in the middle of it where a sea of guys were watching a game of Twister. The participants were also porn stars, oiled up and having a great time by the look of things.

"Hey, Damon!" A few heads turned our way and hands clasped in greeting. "We were wondering if you'd be here."

Damon inclined his head toward me. "We've been taking our time. His first visit to Folsom."

One huge guy in front of us grinned. "Sweet." His gaze met mine. "You'll have a great time." It soon became apparent that we were standing in the middle of seven or eight of Damon's friends, judging by the greetings that flew back and forth. I couldn't help but notice how they addressed him, their voices warm and friendly. I received nods and smiles.

I watched the spectacle, what I could see of it anyway. There had to be hundreds of us, all facing the stage with barely enough room to take one step in any direction.

"Kneel in front of me."

Damon's low instruction broke my concentration. I blinked. "Here?" Damon nodded and I gazed around me in bewilderment. "But… there's no room. We're jammed in here."

Damon grinned. It was as if a ripple started, spreading out from him to all the guys around us. Those in front of him took a step forward, leaving just enough space for me to do as he'd instructed. At his sides, a couple of men shifted closer, their stance almost protective.

How did he do *that?*

"That enough, Damon?" One of the men in front half-inclined his head, his voice low.

"Plenty, thanks, guys." Damon locked gazes with me and pointed to the small clearing they'd created. "Knees, Pete." He gave a quick tug on the leash, still grinning.

No way. I wanted more information before I agreed to… whatever the hell he was suggesting.

"And what am I going to do when I get down there?" My stomach was rock hard but there was a fluttery feeling deep inside it. My heartbeat raced and my skin tingled all over.

"You're going to suck my cock until I come

down your throat." Damon rubbed the crotch of his tight leather pants, where the outline of his erect dick was clearly visible.

I swallowed. It wasn't that I was averse to a little public cocksucking—far from it: my dick would have been like stone at the very idea, if it wasn't for the cock cage Damon had eased and locked around my flaccid member that morning. But not if it was likely to get my ass thrown in jail. "Er, Damon? There are notices everywhere. No sex."

"Pfft. That means nothing." Damon gestured with his head to the tight knit group of guys surrounding us. "They'll tell us if the cops show. And no one in *this* audience is going to complain, trust me." His eyes gleamed. "Or am I pushing you a little too far? Is that it?" He tilted his head to one side. "Because I haven't heard your safe word yet." His lips twitched.

The bastard. He already knew I was going to do it.

I moved to face him, before carefully lowering myself to my knees.

"Good boy." Damon was almost purring. "Hands behind your back, right hand clasping your left wrist."

I did as instructed, Damon's leather pants barely containing his heavy cock inches from my mouth. I licked my lips as he lowered the zip and fished it out, dark with blood, skin stretched tightly over the wide head. He wrapped his hand around the base and held it out at ninety degrees. "Now open wide and take it deep."

Like he needed to tell me twice.

I shut out the crowd, the noise, the possibility of arrest, and sucked on that gorgeous dick. I fucking *loved* the taste of him, had done ever since that first time. Damon was addictive.

He bit back a groan and cupped the back of my head with his hands, holding me steady while he pumped his dick in and out of my mouth, sliding it faster between my lips.

"Fuck, he looks like he's good at that," a voice from beside me whispered.

Damon chuckled. "That mouth is pure gold." He gazed down at me, smiling, and my chest swelled when he stroked the back of my head, his fingers unexpectedly gentle. I resumed my task, determined to do him proud.

"This your boy, Damon?" A deep voice from behind me, the huge guy who'd spoken to me.

My heart hammered, but I kept on licking and sucking the thick cock, my gaze focused on Damon's furred belly, my head bobbing faster.

Damon tugged the hair on the back of my head, jerking my head up, his dick pulling free. When our eyes met, he smiled. "Let's say he's applying for the position."

That did it. If this weekend was my audition, I was going to blow Damon's mind.

Starting with blowing him.

I reapplied myself to the task of giving Damon the best blow job he'd ever received.

"Okay to touch?"

I stuttered in my task but kept on going, eyes straight ahead.

"Be my guest. Just don't fuck him."

I nearly choked on his cock. He pulled free of my mouth and then Damon's fingers were under my chin, lifting it so that I was looking him in the eye. He smiled. "We'll keep that for later, hmm?" he said quietly.

Oh. My. God.

Warm hands stroked their way down my naked back, and I tried not to jump when they reached the swell of my ass. "This looks pretty hot from where I'm standing." I shivered as fingers pressed against the back seam of my shorts. "You going to RD's party tonight?"

"You bet." Damon's eyes locked onto mine, and I couldn't repress the shudder that rippled through me. He guided his cock between my parted lips, and I resumed sucking him, my tongue tracing the heavy vein that ran along the side of his shaft. He nodded in approval again, hips moving fluidly as he glided in and out of my mouth.

"Any chance I can play with him there?"

Damon cackled. "You just want to fuck that hot little ass."

Those hands squeezed my butt. "Damn straight." I almost choked on Damon's dick for the second time when an insistent finger pried its way under the leather, like it was trying to burrow down my crack.

"What's his cock like?"

Damon chuckled. "Sorry, Tate, he's in chastity."

"Aw, fuck."

Damon's gaze was focused on my face as he spoke to Tate. "His hole is all yours, however." He stared at me, and I knew what he was waiting for. My safe word.

As if to confirm my thoughts, Damon pierced me with another hard stare. "That okay with you, Pete?" He pulled back, easing his cock free.

My heart thumped like a car stereo, the bass

turned all the way up. "Yes, Sir." I fought to keep my voice even.

Damon regarded Tate behind me. "He has a tight, hungry little hole that sucks your fingers right in."

That got my heart racing. I breathed heavily, sweat popping out on my forehead as a warm body pressed up against my back and a firm hand slid around my waist to stroke my belly. Lips pressed against my neck, sending shivers through me.

I groaned softly around Damon's fat dick, pleasure trickling through me all the way to my balls.

"Does that feel good?" Damon's voice was low as he continued to thrust into my mouth, an unhurried glide in and out that pushed deeper each time.

I nodded. Speech was out of the question. However, I managed a gasp when two fingers found their way down the back of my loosened shorts, and rubbed over my pucker. I strove to keep still, to concentrate on Damon's cock, but *fuck*, between that and the hot finger tapping against my hole, I was fighting a losing battle.

When a wet finger slowly penetrated my ass, I wanted to cry out because *oh my God*, it felt good. A mouthful of cock solved that issue, which was probably a good thing. The street was by no means quiet, but I was pretty sure the distinctive sound of someone moaning, "Fuck, yeah," loudly would have been a bit of a giveaway that some form of sex was taking place.

"Fuck, he *is* tight, ain't he?" Tate hissed, sliding his finger deeper inside me. Seconds later Damon pulled free and my mouth was invaded by two fingers. "Get them good and wet," Tate instructed.

I complied, but after a second or two he removed them and now two fingers worked their way inside me. My mouth was full of hot, hard cock and Tate began fucking my ass in time with Damon's thrusts. I pushed back, wanting more, moaning softly around the full shaft. When his fingers nudged my sweet spot, I shuddered violently and sucked harder on Damon's dick.

"That's it, boy," Damon praised, hips bucking, his body shaking. "Time we drew this to a close." He seemed breathless, thrusting faster, his dick going deeper. "You're going to swallow what I give you."

I was more than ready to taste his cum again.

But when the moment came, it did so not with a bang but a whimper. Heat filled my shorts as a flood of cum poured from my imprisoned cock, but it was nowhere as satisfying as an orgasm. Slowly Tate removed his fingers and I felt their loss instantly. However, I pushed aside my own feelings of frustration and focused on bringing Damon off. I bobbed my head faster, working his length until his body stiffened. I pulled back slightly when Damon's shaft swelled, his warm cum filling my mouth. I drank every drop, suckling on the head to get the last bit of it, until Damon's harsh breaths told me his dick was too sensitive for me to continue.

Tate's hands rested on my shoulders and warm breath wafted against my ear. "I look forward to seeing this tight little ass at the party tonight," he whispered. Tremors jolted me at the thought of what plans this huge man had for my poor little hole. *Will Damon let him fuck me?* Because right then I wasn't sure I wanted that. Sure, I'd liked the idea all those weeks ago when Damon had suggested sharing me with a group of his friends, but now that it was looking like a possibility…

Then I relaxed. *If I say no, then it's no.* That was the whole point about limits, right?

Damon stroked my cheek and tilted my head up to look at him. "You did well, boy." His eyes were warm.

My heart soared to hear the words. I'd pleased him.

He reached under my pits and hoisted me to my feet before kissing me on the mouth. "I can still taste my cum," he murmured against my lips. "And if you do as well tonight, you get to come." He grinned. "The cage is coming off." When he wrapped his arms around me and held me against his warm body, his hands on my back, I melted into the embrace.

I was determined to do well. I wanted more of this, more of Damon.

And if that meant agreeing to let myself be fucked by his friends, then that was what I'd do.

Anything to keep him in my life.

Party time

Damon

As parties went, it was pretty basic, but it was all that was required. Black vinyl sheets covered the floor, black plastic covered what furniture remained, and RD had set up a couple of slings and two benches. He'd provided condoms, lube, cum towels and bottles of water. Perfect.

As per the invite, it was a 'Bring Your Own Toys' party, not that I'd brought much. Pete kept trying to sneak a peek into my backpack, except he wasn't all that subtle about it.

"You'll see soon enough," I told him with a snicker. I had to admit, he looked damn good. That jock framed his ass cheeks perfectly, and his dick was already straining against it, now free of the cage. The new collar I'd bought from Mr. S looked amazing around his neck, but this time I'd left off the leash.

He was staring at his surroundings, taking it all in. I loved how his eyes lit up when he saw the sling, which was good because I had plans for that. Then he took a *really* good look and froze.

There were maybe ten or eleven guys at the party. Tate, Ray and Jake were already utilizing the sling, and Ray looked like he was in heaven. Jake was in Ray's ass up to his elbow and Ray's loud moans were bouncing off the walls, until Tate stepped up and filled his mouth with a hard cock.

I stepped closer to Pete and leaned in to whisper. "Let's not run before we can walk, hey?" I chuckled.

Jesus. Pete's head jerked round so fast I swore he'd have whiplash. "We're going to do... that?"

I held up one hand and wiggled my fingers at him. "I think this is more than enough to go up your ass, wouldn't you say?"

He nodded so vehemently that I burst out laughing.

"Relax. And besides, Ray has been taking Jake's arm for probably half your lifetime. That works for them. That doesn't mean it works for me, all right?"

"Gotcha." His breathing eased down a notch and he relaxed visibly. I glanced around the room and spied a heavy wooden chair with a padded seat. Exactly what I needed.

"I think you need something to focus you," I said quietly, guiding him toward the chair. I stopped beside it and grinned at him. "How long has it been since I gave you a good spanking?"

I saw the disappointment that flickered in his eyes. It didn't take a genius to work out what he was thinking. *He brings me to a sex party to* spank *me?* I smiled inwardly, doing my best to ignore the fluttery, empty feeling deep in my stomach. *Oh, I have such plans for you, boy.*

"Cat got your tongue? I take it you want to be spanked?"

To his credit, the only words out of his mouth were, "Yes, Sir."

I sat on the chair and gestured to my lap. "Across me."

He lay down over my knees, his crotch between them, his hands reaching down to prop himself up, feet off the floor. I stroked his warm ass, his cheeks round but firm.

"Fuck, that's beautiful." Tate winked at me from across the room. "And you know I want in there later, right?"

I chuckled. "Once I've got it warmed up." Another leisurely rub over both cheeks, before I brought my hand down hard with a loud smack.

"Ugh." Pete's body jolted a little, but he settled back down. I rubbed over where the blow had landed and then smacked the other cheek. For the next five minutes I kept it up, not keeping to a pattern to keep him off balance.

Time to change things up a little.

I pushed at the leg farthest from me, until he bent it and his foot came to rest on the floor. I pulled his cheeks apart and leaned down to blow cool air over his hole, watching the puckered skin tighten. I reached between his spread legs to pull aside his jock and fondle his cock and balls, listening to how the sounds issuing from his lips changed from grunts to soft moans of pleasure. I landed another blow before going right back to squeezing his dick and nuts, alternating between the two activities until he was writhing on my knee.

This time I made sure my smack landed right over his crack. He shuddered, and I rubbed gently over his hole with my middle finger, earning me a low, primal noise of appreciation. I gripped his cock while I spanked him, blow after blow, feeling his length jerk and stiffen with each smack.

"Yeah, you like this, don't you?" I gave him a particularly hard crack, where his ass met the top of his thigh.

"Y-yes, sir," he stammered out. When I did it again, he grunted and tilted his ass high as if begging for more.

I didn't want it to be said that I didn't give my boy what he needed.

By the time I was done spanking him, his cheeks were bright red. Except I knew I wasn't finished.

"Stand up," I instructed him. "And take off that jock."

Pete clambered off my knee and hurriedly removed it. He stood in front of me, his cock rigid and poking straight up.

I grinned. "Yeah, you really did like that, didn't you?" Pete did that adorable flush of his.

"Lord, look at that." Jake whistled. "Bet that ass is toasty warm right now." He stood beside Ray while he wiped down his arm. Ray was looking blissed out, lying limp on the sling bed.

I snickered. "Yeah, and I'm not done with it yet." I slapped my thighs. "Bring your ass right here, boy." When Pete frowned, I smiled. "Ever play wheelbarrow when you were a kid? That's what I want, your ass right in front of me, your legs on either side of my waist, your thighs on mine."

He turned his back to me and crouched, lifting one leg at a time until he was leaning on his forearms, legs spread wide, and that gorgeous ass right where I wanted it.

I couldn't resist.

I spread those firm cheeks, bent over as far as I could and licked slowly over his hole.

"Oh fuck," he said softly, his body trembling, his head lowering to the vinyl covered floor.

I wanted more of those soft moans, those low cries of pleasure. I wanted to get him to the point where Pete was begging me to fuck him.

I prized those downy cheeks apart and stretched his hole wide, before dipping again to plunge my tongue into its heat. Then I did it again. And again. And again, until Pete was shaking, his cries louder. Only then did I sink a finger into that dark warmth, aiming for his gland.

Pete shuddered. "Fuck, yeah," he groaned, pushing back, chasing the sensation.

"Yeah, you like it when I finger you." I reached down to where his solid dick pointed toward the floor, and grasped it around the base. Pete jerked his hips to fuck my hand, until I squeezed him tightly. "Be still."

He froze, his breathing loud and uneven. I held onto his thick shaft and proceeded to fuck his hole with my finger, his tremors growing more pronounced with every slide of my fingertip over his prostate. I kept it up for as long as I could, before slowly pulling free and leaving him there on my lap, still shaking.

"Throw me some lube, Tate?" For what I intended, spit wouldn't be enough.

Tate tossed me a packet. When I'd slicked up my fingers, I eased two of them into Pete's still tight channel. He shuddered, his ass pushing back toward me, and I chuckled. "Greedy boy. Patience." I fucked him with them for a minute or two, loving the sounds that poured out of him, the obvious moans of satisfaction. When I added a third, he stiffened for a moment, before relaxing and meeting each glide of my fingers deep into his rectum.

I paused and bent over his ass. "Want to try a fourth?"

Pete's groan was answer enough.

Keeping my thumb free, I eased four fingers

into him, taking my time. It was a tight fit, but after a while his hole loosened, and I was able to gently move them in and out of him.

I stilled, my fingers resting inside his warm ass. "Does that feel good?"

Pete tried to twist around to look at me, but I growled out, "Eyes forward." His head dropped back to the floor, his shoulders hunched over. "And you didn't answer my question."

"It feels fucking good, just don't keep stopping!" The words burst out of him.

I let out a cackle. "Who's in charge here?" I moved my fingers, filling him until the tip of my thumb was almost in there too. "Look at that beautiful hole, stretched wide for me. One day it'll be my hand inside you, fucking you."

"God, you're such a fucking *tease*!"

I slid them in and out, the sound slick and wet. "You're like hot silk inside there, boy." A little faster, rougher than before. Pete's hips bucked and he moaned.

He moaned even louder when I stopped and withdrew my finger, leaving his hole stretched and gaping.

He was ready for my surprise.

My hole felt so empty.

I ached for Damon to fill it again, but he'd gone quiet on me. I didn't dare turn around, not after the first time. All I could do was wait, my body taut, my skin tingling all over.

"Remember when you had me tied to your bed, Petey-boy?"

Oh… fuck.

"Yeah," I replied cautiously. Ice trickled down my spine. *Oh God, it's payback time.*

"Remember how much you enjoyed fucking me with that dildo? That long, thick dildo?" He sounded gleeful. That was when I knew I was in for it—or at least my ass was.

Before I could think of how to respond, something nudged my hole. Something slick and cold—and big.

"Breathe," Damon said quietly. "Let your ass take it in."

Whatever he was aiming to fuck me with was unyielding. It was cold and hard, like…

"That's a glass dildo, isn't it?" I breathed deeply, trying to relax, and was rewarded when the dildo slid into my slick channel. Fuck, I could feel how it stretched me wide. I was so full.

Damon said nothing, but instead he inched the dildo a little farther inside me. Goosebumps broke out over my arms and chest. "Why does that feel… different?" I'd used a dildo before, but it had never sent waves of pleasure breaking over me.

"That would be the little bumps all over it." He slid it deeper, and I pushed out a loud groan when it nudged my sweet spot. "There we go." I could hear the smile in his voice.

The urge to say another word left me when Damon began to fuck me with the dildo, and I met his thrusts, wanting more. The hairs on my arms stood on end and my breath left me in short, harsh bursts. I couldn't push back hard enough: all I wanted to do was impale myself on that solid glass phallus and have it slide over my gland again and again. But my position rendered that possibility null and void, and I was forced to take what he gave me.

One glance told me we were the center of attention. All other activity had ceased as the men stood around, their eyes fixed on the pair of us. Ray was out of the sling and leaning against Jake, still looking like he was out of it.

"Let me hear you," Damon called out, bringing my attention back to him.

"What do you want to hear?" I panted. "How much I wish it was your cock inside me, instead of a piece of cold, hard glass?" It felt good, felt fantastic—but it wasn't Damon.

His hand was warm on my ass, stroking and squeezing me, while he fucked me faster, those bumps on the glass shaft sending sparks dancing up and down my spine, sending me higher.

Tate squatted in front of me, his fingers gripping my chin to tilt my head upward. With his other hand he held out his dick, fatter than Damon's, pre-come dripping from the slit. "How about this? Want to feel *this* reaming that tight ass?"

I shivered, unable to suppress the reaction. My body jerked forward when Damon gave a particularly hard shove into me, punching the air from my lungs. When he pulled it free of my ass, I wanted to howl with frustration.

"On your feet, and get your ass over to that sling."

I was too busy scrambling off his lap to punch the air.

Tate lifted me bodily and lowered me onto the wide leather bed of the sling. I was dying to thank him, but I knew he was only thinking with his dick. He stroked over my chest and belly, before wrapping large, thick fingers around my shaft. When he trailed his hand lower over my sac, I tensed.

Damon was on it.

"You can stop right there." His voice had an edge to it that I'd not heard before, and I shivered. Damon's hands were warm on my ankles as they fastened the stirrups in place, supporting my legs.

Tate stood beside me, his wide cock jutting out. "Do we get a taste?"

My eyes were on Damon as I waited for him to ask me, as I knew he would.

I never got the chance.

Damon gazed down at me, his hand leisurely caressing my calf. My heart pounded as I waited, my breathing staccato.

He smiled at me, the kind of smile that always turned my insides to jelly. "No, not tonight," he said finally, not once looking in Tate's direction. "Tonight Pete is all mine."

There were groans of disappointment that should have gratified me, but all I felt was sweeping relief.

"Here." Jake tossed Damon a condom. "But you're not gonna stop me from watching you plow his ass."

"Be my guest," Damon said with a chuckle while he gloved up and then wiped a lube-slick hand over his dick. He placed himself between my spread legs and guided the head of his cock into position. I could feel its heat against my hole. Our gazes locked. "Ready to get fucked?"

All I could think of was the last time he'd been inside me. That had not been fucking. It had felt for all the world like he was making love to me. And much as I loved it when Damon took me roughly, I yearned to feel what I'd experienced the night of his mom's party.

There was something missing, something vital.

Then it hit me.

"Kiss me?" My voice shook.

Damon smiled and bent over to take my mouth in an all-consuming kiss, his tongue easing between my lips to explore me, taste me. I let go of the chains and wrapped my arms around him, holding his firm, hairy body against mine. He grabbed hold of the chains at my shoulders and slowly entered me while we kissed, unhurried.

I pushed a soft sigh between his lips. "Fuck, yeah. You feel so good inside me."

He stilled, raised his head and our eyes met. "Are you my boy, Pete?"

I swallowed. "Yours, Sir. All of me." I meant every single fucking word. I wanted to belong to him, heart, body and soul, like I'd never wanted anything my entire life.

Damon's face glowed. "Then it looks like I've got myself a boy." He eased out of me and my heartbeat raced. "Hold on to the chains."

I grabbed the leather straps that hung from them, my breathing rapid.

He thrust back into me, filling me to the hilt, and I groaned. Damon grinned. "Time to claim this ass as mine."

Before I had time to draw breath, he slammed into me, cock going deep, and commenced fucking me with a steady rhythm. Within minutes I was crying out, my dick so hard it ached. Damon continued his relentless fuck, each time driving his cock into me until he was balls deep. I swear he hit my gland with every thrust.

"Damon, oh, fuck, Sir…" They were about the only words that made any sense.

His hips snapped forward, his dick pistoning in and out of my ass, setting me on fire with each slam into me. His eyes were focused on my face, his cheeks flushed, his body glistening with sweat. My nostrils were filled with his musk, the smell of cum and the raw odor of sex.

Above me, Damon gripped the chains and shoved deep into my ass, his body stiffening. Inside me his cock swelled and he came with a harsh cry. I could feel every throb of his shaft as it pulsed into the latex, and it was this that sent me over the edge with no need to touch my dick.

I trembled as warm cum spattered my torso, some reaching as far as my cheek. Damon let go of the chains and bent over to kiss me, drops of sweat from his brow landing onto my face and chest. His hand curved around my cheek and he stared into my eyes. "Mine." His fingers traced the leather collar around my neck.

I reached up to cover his hand with my own. "Yours."

It didn't matter in that moment that it wasn't enough. I was Damon's boy, and that would have to do. I pushed aside my innermost desires and smiled at him, not wishing him to even glimpse what lay beneath the smile.

He wanted a boy.

I wanted Damon. All of him. Twenty-four seven.

WTF?

Damon

I pulled the car into the driveway and switched off the engine. The street was quiet and dark, not surprising given the hour. Sunday night and the world lay sleeping, readying itself for the start of a new week.

I didn't want my night to end.

Pete had been silent the whole trip back to my place. At first I wasn't concerned. I figured he was still blissed out after the fucking in the sling. But something about the atmosphere inside the car niggled me.

I knew why I hadn't noticed. I'd been lost in my own thoughts, ever since we'd left RD's and walked to where I'd left the car. For the first time in a very long while, I wanted someone in my life.

There were times when I told myself I was happier on my own. No hassles, no one to bug me, no one to upset my routines. But there were also times when I wanted more than my own company. I knew why I shied away from the idea of a relationship. Once bitten, twice shy, was a damn good proverb to live by, and I was all too aware how accurate it was. I'd been there, after all.

A shiver coursed through me. *Damn him.* All these years since he'd been a part of my life and Michael still haunted me.

"Are you okay?" Pete's hesitant question broke through.

I could hear the genuine note of concern in his voice, a voice that I was steadily growing more accustomed to hearing.

Fuck it. Why was I wasting time? There was a gorgeous man next to me, one who was becoming increasingly more interesting and more important to me. What was the point in being stubborn? What did it get me, apart from loneliness?

My house stood before us, dark and empty. It didn't have to be that way.

All I had to do was open my mouth and...

I switched on the light above our heads before twisting in my seat to face him. "Thank you for coming with me today."

Pete's face lit up. "Thanks for asking me. It was... awesome. And the party was definitely an experience."

I laughed. "A good one, I hope."

He chuckled. "An eye-opener, to say the least." He regarded me in silence, his blond hair almost white in the stark light. "Damon, I..." He stopped, his teeth worrying his lip.

I knew the signs. Funny how quickly I'd gotten to know his quirks and foibles.

"Tell me what's on your mind."

Pete blinked. "Oh, it's nothing, really."

It didn't look like nothing.

The weirdest thought flitted across my mind. *What if he feels the same? How strange would that be?* I pushed it aside. I'd known what Pete had wanted ever since he'd knelt beside his bed and called me Sir. Well, he'd gotten what he wanted.

Too bad I wanted more.

For fuck's sake. Grow a pair and tell him how you feel.

I was always one to go with my gut.

I reached across and cupped his cheek. The

hitch in his breathing got my heartbeat racing.

"Pete, about tonight." I took a deep breath and prepared to step out into the dark. "How would you feel about spending the night with me?" I didn't want him to go home. I wanted him in my bed, in my arms, all night long. I ran through my mental diary for the following days' appointments and grinned inwardly. I'd be taking a day off and hoping he could do the same.

I wanted time with him. Maybe if I got that, I'd be able to say what I *really* wanted.

"I think that sounds wonderful," he said softly. "Do you have to get up early tomorrow?"

I smiled. "Actually, I was thinking of taking a day off tomorrow. The perks of being self-employed."

Fuck, that smile…. Hook him up to a generator and it could have powered every street light on the block.

"I don't have a job on until Tuesday," he told me. "And ditto with the whole self-employment thing."

"Perfect," I whispered, before leaning over to kiss him on the lips. He made a soft noise of contentment and his arm slipped around me, pulling me closer. I deepened the kiss, exploring his mouth with my tongue, savoring the taste of him, the way he smelled, a warm scent that stirred something deep in my belly.

Light flooded the car as the security light under the porch burst into life.

I blinked and peered through the windshield, trying to see.

"Damon, there's someone on your porch," Pete said in a low voice.

I frowned. "At this time of night?" Quickly I unfastened my seatbelt, Pete doing the same, and we got out of the car. I locked it and strode toward the house, Pete at my side. "Who's there?" I called out.

"You always did keep unsociable hours."

The deep voice sent a lance through me. It couldn't be. I blinked and shaded my eyes, just as a tall, lean figure stepped out from under the porch.

Holy Fucking Hell.

He was older than the last time I'd seen him, but then so was I.

"Michael?" My voice came out winded. "What the fuck are you doing here?"

FRACTURES

TANTALUS

FRACTURES

Pete doesn't know where he stands when Damon's ex, Michael, turns up out of the blue.
Talk about bad timing.
Damon had thought his wounds long since healed. Yeah, right.
So where do they go from here?

FRACTURES

WTF?

Damon

"I'm not upsetting your plans, am I?" Michael asked with a smirk. "From where I was, it looked like I'd interrupted something." He looked me up and down. "Nice outfit."

Fuck him. I knew he was angling to know who Pete was—and more importantly, who he was to me—but Michael had lost that right years ago. "It's late, Michael." About eighteen years too late, if I were honest.

"Too late to come in for a drink and catch up a little? Come on, just one drink."

I arched my eyebrows. "For old times' sake?" I still couldn't believe he was standing there. He wore his hair a damn sight shorter than he had back in college, and he'd put on a few pounds, but little else had changed, apart from the lines around his eyes.

That smirk sure hadn't.

Then I realized he hadn't given Pete so much as a glance, and I bristled. I turned to Pete and put my hand on his arm. "Go home. I'll be over there shortly." I faked a smile I certainly didn't feel: I didn't want Pete worrying.

Yeah. Fat chance of that.

Pete's gaze went from me to Michael. "If you're sure." God, he held himself so stiffly. Not that I blamed him. I'd deliberately kept my tone devoid of emotion, and while he didn't deserve that after the amazing day we'd shared, I didn't want to give away too much about our relationship.

That was none of Michael's goddamn business.

I nodded. "I'll be fine. I won't be long." I didn't want to make it more forceful than that, hoping he'd go along with it. I'd explain everything later.

Pete gave Michael one final glance, then nodded slowly. He cut across the lawn, heading for his front door. I waited until he was inside before giving Michael my attention.

"One drink, huh?"

He shrugged. "Something like that, I guess. Plus, I want to find out what you've done with your life since college."

It was on the tip of my tongue to yell, 'Well, you'd fucking *know* that if you hadn't left, wouldn't ya?' It took all my effort to choke back the words. Like I wasn't curious to know what he'd been doing all these years too.

"You'd better come in then."

One drink was all he was gonna get. Right then I had a boy to hold, a boy who had to be going out of his mind. I wasn't stupid. Pete had heard Michael's name at Mama's birthday party, when I'd been talking to Max, so he knew Michael was some kind of ex, and that he'd been important.

Fuck, your timing sucks, Michael.

I opened the front door and stood to one side

to let him enter. I snuck a glance next door, just in time to see the blinds twitch in the front window. My heart sank. What had to be going through Pete's mind? After the day we'd shared, the... connection between us, he had to be wondering what the fuck was going on.

Well, so was I.

I closed the door behind me and bolted it. Michael was standing awkwardly in the hallway, so I indicated the living room. "Go on through." He wasn't the only one who needed a drink. I followed him into the room, and headed for the liquor cabinet. "I got whiskey, rum and vodka. Not sure about mixers." I wasn't a big drinker: I got my highs in other ways.

"Whiskey will be fine. Neat."

I pulled down two squat glasses, and poured about two fingers of whiskey into each one. I handed a glass to Michael, then ignored the empty seat cushion beside him on the couch, and sat in the armchair beside the fireplace. His face tightened, but I didn't give a shit. He'd burned his bridges with me a long time ago. Right then all I wanted was answers.

Michael took a sip of whiskey and settled back against the cushions. "You've got a nice place here," he said, glancing around the room.

"Nope." I shook my head. "We are *not* doing small talk. You don't get to waltz in here after eighteen years and act like this is a social visit."

"Can't I just take a little time and work up to the Q&A?" he joked.

I took a long drink, then put down my glass. "No, you fucking don't," I enunciated carefully. "Eighteen fucking *years*, Michael." My voice rose, cracking a little.

He blinked. "I don't remember you as someone who swore a lot."

"Yeah, well, I'm not the same guy you walked out on. I've changed. Your leaving had a lot to do with that." And wasn't *that* the truth?

Michael winced. "Jeez, d'you have to sound so dramatic? You're acting like I disappeared without a word. I wrote you a letter, explaining everything."

I clenched my fists, forcing myself to breathe, but it was no good. All the rage and humiliation, all the hurt and anguish he'd put me through, that I'd stomped on, pushed down, buried as fucking deep as it would go, was bubbling to the surface, like it had never been away.

"One lousy letter. One *fucking* letter, saying you'd got this fantastic job lined up on the east coast, and wasn't it a great opportunity? One letter, saying thanks for everything we'd shared, and how you were sure I'd meet someone who'd make me happy. Well, I got news for ya, pal. I *was* fucking happy—with *you*, right up until the moment I discovered exactly how much I meant to you."

Michael sighed heavily. "You were always way more into me than I was into you."

God, if I'd been next to him, I think I'd have throttled the life out of him.

"Three years, Michael. We were together three fucking years. Don't you think you owed me more than one letter? Christ, that last semester before we graduated, we were making plans. We were gonna live together."

"And that right there is why I took the job in New York!" he shouted.

Damon & Pete: Playing with Fire

I froze. "What? What the hell does that mean?"

"We were twenty-two, for God's sake!" Michael's eyes were wide, his cheeks flushed. He dragged in a couple of deep breaths, visibly growing calmer. "Damon, you were getting really serious. It was... stifling, sometimes. And the closer we got to graduation, the more you talked about our future."

"Because I thought we had one," I gritted out. "Because I thought we were in love." Only now I was seeing things clearly. I'd been in love with him. Whereas Michael?

I sagged into the armchair as the reality struck with all the force of a sledgehammer.

"You didn't love me, did you?"

Michael's mouth fell open, the flush on his chest and neck deepening, visible beneath his shirt, open at the collar. "I... I thought I did, at first. I mean, we were crazy hot together, right?"

I said nothing. I wasn't about to deny it. The sex had been phenomenal.

Except... I'd thought we were more than that. Apparently not.

"I guess I got cold feet," he said simply. "I'd applied for the job in New York, not really thinking they'd be interested in someone with the ink barely drying on his degree. But they really liked me."

"Why didn't you tell me any of this? Especially the part about getting cold feet. Instead of leaving the way you did? Didn't you think that was gonna hurt me?" Now it all made sense. Why he always seemed reluctant when I talked about our plans for after graduation. I'd already decided where I wanted to go with my life. Psychology had been one of my strongest subjects, and I knew I wanted some kind of career in therapy. The sexology part had come later, born out of a burgeoning interest in relationships.

Born out of what had started in the aftermath of Michael's exit.

"You must have known at graduation that you already had the job, yet you said nothing."

"I was going to, I swear."

"But you *didn't*," I stressed. "You left at the end of the semester, went home—and mailed me a letter. I called you. God, I lost count of how many times a day I called you after I read it. But you didn't answer. I called your parents, but all they'd tell me was you'd moved to New York. No forwarding address, even though I begged them for it. I fucking *begged*, Michael." Christ, the pain I'd thought was long gone was *right there,* constricting my chest, knotting up my insides, and making my head ache.

"If it means anything, my folks gave me a lot of shit about how I treated you."

"Good," I blurted out. "Now tell me why you're here." When he blinked again, I speared him with a look. "It's been eighteen years and you just decide to pay me a visit on a whim? At this hour? Not buying it. For one thing, you found where I'm living. That speaks of intent. So why now?"

He swallowed. "I guess I owe you that much. And I'm sorry about being here so late. I've been sitting on your porch for hours, hoping to God you hadn't gone away or something. I was gonna give it another hour when you showed up." He took a breath before continuing. "I'm still in New York, still working with the same company, and… I met someone."

"Good for you," I said bitterly. "You'd better

Damon & Pete: Playing with Fire

not be here to invite me to your fucking wedding, because you do that, and I'll spit in your face, so help me God. Even you wouldn't be that crass."

His face fell. "There'll be no wedding. He..." He closed his eyes and bowed his head.

Something deep in my stomach roiled. As much as I didn't want him to be happy, to make up for all the shit he'd put me through, I hated the idea that I'd made that last remark about a guy who'd died. That seemed... petty. Mean.

Michael raised his chin. "He left me, a couple of months ago. After ten years together. He left me for someone else."

For a moment, I was nonplussed. "I don't understand." What the fuck did that have to do with me?

Michael drained his glass, wincing briefly. "I've been seeing a therapist. I wasn't coping well after Nate left. I wasn't sleeping, I had no appetite, and eventually I figured I needed help. One of the things that came up in my therapy sessions was you. More importantly, how I'd treated you."

Oh my fucking God. "Closure? You came here for closure? You finally got to be on the receiving end, and it made you realize what you'd put me through?"

Judging by his startled expression, I'd nailed it.

I got up and walked over to where he sat, staring down at his upturned face. "What did you think was gonna happen, Michael? You were gonna walk in here, ask for forgiveness for treating me like shit, and I'd put my arms around you and say, 'there there, baby, it'll be all right?' I mean, really?" I gazed at him in disbelief. "You have no fucking idea, do you, of what you put me through? How you made me doubt every relationship that followed, because I always wondered what the hell I'd done to make you leave like that? How I hated the fact that *every single thing* about your exit from my life was beyond my control?"

That was the one blessing to come out of that horrific episode. The need for control. To be the one in control. Not that I was about to share that knowledge with Michael.

Then it hit me. I finally had the answer to the mystery of Michael's disappearance. This was *over*. I could leave the years of wondering and doubt behind me, and move on. Because now there was someone in my life who had the potential to mean more to me than Michael ever had.

There was a boy next door who needed me. A boy *I* needed, like air.

"I'm sorry he left you. I'm glad you finally realize what it feels like to be hurt. Really hurt. I'm glad you're getting help." I breathed in deeply, then expelled a long, drawn-out sigh. "But I'm not gonna forgive you. Not that you've even asked to be forgiven." I tilted my head to one side. "But that's not why you're here, is it? You didn't come to apologize or ask forgiveness. You just came to make yourself feel better." Michael stiffened, and I knew I'd hit my mark. "Right now you need to leave. I don't expect to see you again." Another breath shuddered out of me. "I'm sorry if it's not the outcome you expected, but right now? I don't give a fuck. I have a life to lead, and you're not in it." Then I relented. I could afford to be civil, right? After all, I had Pete.

I softened my voice. "Goodbye, Michael."

Michael gaped at me liked I'd lost my mind, and I stared right back at him. Finally, his shoulders slumped. "I deserve that, I guess." He got to his feet and handed me the empty glass, before walking dejectedly toward the front door. When he got there, he waited for me to unbolt it. He glanced down at my leather pants and vest, my shiny black boots. "You never did explain the outfit. Or tell me what you're doing now."

"And I'm not going to," I said quietly, trying my damnedest to keep a lid on my emotions. I felt... stretched, like any second all hell was going to break loose.

Michael opened his mouth as if to add something, and I held out my hand. We shook, which was about as civil as I was capable of being right then. I watched him walk slowly along the driveway, past my car, and turn left onto the street. I waited until he was no longer in sight, before sagging against the door frame, wrung out.

Out of the corner of my eye, I caught movement, and turned my head in time to see another twitch of Pete's blinds. I locked my front door and cut across the lawn to Pete's house.

I had unfinished business with Pete.

After The Party's Over...

Pete

I glanced at the clock for what had to be the twentieth time, and tried not to think about what was going on in Damon's house. I'd already peeked through the blinds two or three times, before forcing myself to step away from the window. As the minutes passed, I told myself a lengthy conversation was to be expected. What little I knew about Michael led me to think it had been many years since he and Damon had seen each other. Of *course* they had a lot to discuss.

I was trying very hard *not* to think about Michael being Damon's ex. And even harder not to recall Damon's dismissal of me. Because that was what it had felt like. A fucking dismissal, and it was robbing me of every joyful moment I'd experienced. Up until the moment when that damn porch light came on, the whole weekend had seemed... idyllic. Awesome. Amazing. All of it. Shopping for leather. Sucking Damon's cock on my knees in the middle of a crowded street, while a complete stranger fingered my ass. And that goddamn party...

As exhilarating as it had been to have Damon fuck me in that sling, my heart pounding as I waited to find out whether he'd allow one of his friends to join in or not, one moment stuck in my mind, and I couldn't shake it. Those fragile minutes before that porch light had blinked into existence. That bubble of time when I'd been *this* close to telling Damon how I really felt about him. If he was serious about me being his boy, that was great—only, I wanted more.

And I was scared to death in case I asked him for what I wanted, and the answer was no. Him sending me home like that was only adding to my fears. Then I pushed aside that thought. It only got me riled up. Logic told me Damon had to have a reason for speaking to me like that.

I really wanted to believe that.

Funny how this had all started. A bet I'd been determined to lose, if it got me what I wanted—Damon, in whatever way I could have him. The kinky side of me rejoiced at the direction events had taken, but there was more to it now than the kink. There was the night in Damon's bed, that had been so far removed from a fuck, it was unreal. Damon had shaken me to my core, and left me with a hunger I'd never experienced.

Another glance at the clock. *How much longer are they gonna talk?* My bag was still in the trunk of Damon's car, my leather gear inside it. I was grateful I'd changed into a pair of sweats before we'd left the party. Damon had snickered at me not wanting to walk out to his car in my teeny leather jock. That collar was still around my neck, however, and I wanted it to stay there.

One more peek through the blinds. Forget about that damn watched pot… Only this time, Damon's porch light was on again, and there was movement. I let go of the blind and stepped away in a hurry. I didn't want him to think I'd been spying on him. Besides, just because it looked like Michael was leaving, didn't necessarily mean Damon was gonna come straight over here, right?

When I caught the sound of feet on the gravel path, my heart raced. *Finally*. I was at the door by the time he'd finished knocking, yanking it open, my

Damon & Pete: Playing with Fire

hands clammier than they had been seconds before. Damon stood there in his leather pants and vest, hands by his sides, his expression...

Oh God. His eyes. Such a look of naked pain.

"Are you okay?" I stood aside to let him enter and closed the door after him, cursing myself for asking such a pointless question. Of course he wasn't okay. Any fool could see that. Then all such thoughts fled as Damon invaded my space, his body pressing me against the wall, his lips seeking mine, his hands on my face.

I didn't question why. I melted into his kiss, opening for him, welcoming the ferocity of that sensual assault. I wanted to drop to my knees, bury my face in his belly, and wrap my arms around him, clinging to him, with the intention of never letting go. My head hit the wall with a dull thud, and still he kissed me, his tongue exploring my mouth, hands gripping the sides of my head to hold me there.

Like I wanted to be anywhere else.

Damon broke the kiss with an abruptness that stole my breath, pulled back, and looked me in the eye. "Christ, I need you." He traced the line of my collar with his fingertips.

"You got me," I breathed. "Take what you need."

He stilled. "Boy, I intend to." He grabbed my wrist and pinned it against the wall above my head, before taking the other wrist and doing the same. He pressed his body against mine, and his lips claimed my mouth in another searing kiss. Fuck, the heat from him... I moaned into his kiss, wanting more. When he paused and stared into my eyes again, the skin on the back of my neck prickled.

"Remember the other day when we talked

about limits? Trust? Testing?"

I nodded, swallowing.

"I'm negative. You're negative."

Holy fuck. I couldn't breathe.

Damon speared me with an intense gaze. "Silence is not consent. You know better."

Oh God. I dragged air into my lungs. "Fuck me, sir. Fuck me bare." What breath I had was punched out of me when he spun me around to face the wall, pushing me against it. I pressed my palms flat to the painted surface, my head turned so my cheek met the cool plaster, shivering as he yanked down my sweats, all the way to my ankles. I caught the unmistakable sound of a zipper being lowered— and the equally distinctive sound of him spitting.

Damon's breath warmed the back of my neck. "That's all you're getting. I figure you're still slick enough in there. It wasn't that long ago I was inside you." He swatted my thigh. "Put your foot up on that chair arm. Spread yourself."

My skin erupted in a swathe of goosebumps as I complied with his instructions, kicking off my sweats and pushing my ass out toward him in anticipation of the penetration I knew was coming. He didn't make me wait long before Damon's hot, bare cock pushed slowly but insistently between my cheeks, not stopping until he was buried in me up to the hilt, his fat dick stretching my hole. Damon's hand was on my neck, holding me still while he gave a couple of leisurely strokes in and out of me, the initial burn fading quickly.

His breath tickled my ear. "This hole is mine," he ground out, before placing his foot next to mine on the chair and stabbing his cock into my body in a sharp thrust. He slammed his body against me, fucking me with short, quick jabs. The only sounds were my own cries and the harsh slapping of flesh against flesh. Damon pushed my head to the wall, his other hand on my hip as he pulled me back onto his dick to meet his thrusts. The zipper bit into my ass cheek with every stroke into my hole, I slammed into the wall as his body connected with mine—and it was fucking *glorious.*

"Fuck, yeah," I groaned. "Fucking *use* me." If this was how he wanted me, no more than a hole for his cock, then he could have me. I was his, body, heart and soul.

Damon slowed down, his lips on my shoulder as he kissed me there, before biting gently, the pain just shy of exquisite. I tried to turn my head further to meet his lips, but he held me steady, still pinned against the wall. He kissed me again, an unexpectedly soft brushing of lips against my neck. "Time for me to come in this ass," he said quietly. Then it was back to fucking me, filling me with his hot shaft as he set up a punishing rhythm, not slowing once. His hand stayed on my head, holding me there while he sped up, slamming into me faster and faster, grunting with each thrust, the sounds growing louder and harsher, until I knew he was there.

Damon speared me with his cock, and I felt it throb, the first time I'd ever had someone shoot their load inside me without a rubber. All my worries about Michael, all my fears and doubts, ebbed away as Damon covered me with his body, his hands over mine, and still I felt him pulse inside me. I didn't matter that I hadn't gotten off. I wasn't stupid. This was for Damon.

His breathing slowed, his chest slick against

my back. "Mine," he murmured, kissing my shoulder again.

"Yours." I took hold of his hand and brought it to the collar around my neck. The collar he'd placed there. "Yours," I repeated.

Like there was ever any doubt.

His cock still wedged inside me, Damon leaned forward to kiss me on the mouth, one of those sideways kisses that always looks awkward when you see it, but one that I'd craved ever since I'd felt that first warm load inside me.

When he eased his dick out of me, I shuddered as he slid a finger into my now aching hole. "Gimme that cum."

I pushed it out of me, and Damon dropped to his knees behind me, pulling my cheeks apart as he buried his face between them, his warm tongue lapping my hole, licking over my sac where his cum had trickled down. His stubble scratched my ass, his tongue soothed my well-used hole, while he kept me spread with his fingers. When he was done, Damon got to his feet and turned me around.

I didn't wait for further instructions, but put my arms around his neck and kissed him deeply, the taste of his cum still on his lips. Damon returned the kiss, clutching the sides of my head as though preventing my escape.

Yeah right. I was where I wanted to be. I wanted to ask if he was feeling better, but some innate sense told me to keep quiet.

Damon broke the kiss and gazed at me, his brow furrowed, and my heart sank. *We're not out of the woods yet.*

"Pete, I..." He swallowed.

For a moment I was lost, until it hit me. *Oh*

my fucking God. Damon's nervous. I froze, my stomach churning, unsure what was coming right at me. One thought struck me, and I went cold. *Don't tell me that was a goodbye fuck.* Then I reasoned I was being stupid. *He said I was his, didn't he? So whatever he's got to say to me, it sure isn't 'Adios, Pete'.*

"I love you."

I blinked. I blinked again. My brain didn't seem to want to fire. "You…" I lapsed into silence. Whatever I'd expected, that was not it.

Damon tilted his head to one side. "You're gonna make me say it again, aren't ya?"

"Only because I think I was dreaming the first time, because for a minute there, it sounded like you said you love me."

Damon snorted. "I can spank your ass *and* love you at the same time, you know that, right?"

There was my Damon. "I'm counting on it." But I couldn't leave him hanging, not when he'd just taken a huge step outside his comfort zone. "And I can take whatever you have to give, and love you too."

God, he was so still. "You mean that?"

My arms were locked around his neck, so I pulled him a little closer. "That's what I wanted to say earlier, before we got… interrupted." Closer. "I love you. Yes, I want to be your boy, but I want to be your man too, whether or not I'm wearing your collar." Our lips were almost touching. "Do you want that too?" Fuck, I was trembling, and my head was reeling. This was…. Damon, telling me he loved me. Damon, acting like he couldn't believe I loved him back.

"Fuck, yes." Then his lips collided with

mine, and I melted once again into a toe-curling kiss, only this one was different.

This was a kind of seal-the-deal kiss, and I knew it.

Even those kinds of kisses have to end eventually. Damon drew back with a sigh. "Okay. We need to clean up."

"And then?"

He smiled. "And then we sit on the couch, and we have a talk. I need to tell you about tonight, but… I can do that now."

"Because you fucked your anger away?" I joked.

He shook his head. "Because now you know how I feel. And if we're going to make this work, then we both need to know where we're going."

"Limits?" I said with a smile.

He laughed softly. "Exactly." He reached down and smacked my ass. "Bathroom. Now."

I attempted to glare at him. "Excuse me? Whose house is this?"

He grabbed my butt and squeezed it. "Whose ass is this?"

"Yours." I had no argument on that score.

Damon nodded smugly. "Then whether it's your house or mine, what I say goes."

When he put it like that…

"Yes, Sir." The words came out quietly, but I uttered them with all my heart.

A Time To Talk

Damon

It had been a long time since I'd shared a shower with a guy and we'd not ended up fucking, but I had to admit, I liked it. Pete washed me with a care that was almost reverential, and my throat tightened. I told myself it had just been an emotional night, that I was tired…

That was total bullshit. This guy had gotten under my skin and into my heart in a way no man had done since—

Nope. I wasn't gonna think about him. Not when there was a beautiful man in my arms, who'd just told me he loved me. There was no contest.

When we were dry, and wrapped up in a couple of robes, I led Pete into the living room, sat on the couch, and patted my lap. "On your back, your head here."

Pete moved slowly, taking his time to get comfortable. When he was ready, his feet resting on the far arm of the couch, I stroked his hair. "Thanks for staying up for me."

He gave me an incredulous glance. "You think I could've gone to bed, not knowing what was happening?"

I gazed down at him. "Were you worried?" He fell silent, and I stroked his cheek. "Tell me the truth."

"A little. I mean, I know you said I was your boy, but then I knew he was your ex, and turning up like that…" His brow smoothed out. "You wanna know when I stopped worrying? When you fucked me raw. That said… fuck, that said so much."

"Which was exactly what I intended. I wanted you to have no doubts. And that leads us neatly to our discussion… what happens next." I smiled. "This is the part where you tell me what *you* want out of this, where *you* want this to go. It's not me doing all the talking. There are two people in this room."

Christ, it was like he'd become a statue.

"Pete?" I cupped his chin, staring into his eyes.

Finally, he let out a sigh. "It's not that I don't know what I want. It's just that I'm…"

Then I got it. "You're scared to tell me." When he nodded, I closed my eyes. Not exactly what I'd hoped for.

"Sir?" His fingers met mine in a tentative gesture. I opened my eyes and looked at him. Pete took a deep breath. "I want to be your boy. One thing I've learned since we started this, is that I want to submit to you. Everything we've done so far has been… awesome. But…"

"But?"

His gaze locked on mine, and he swallowed. "I want more than that. I don't want to come over to your place for a session in your basement or your bedroom, then come back here and get on with my life, waiting for the next time. I want to be a part of *your* life." He didn't break eye contact. "I want to wake up in the morning either at your side or on the floor beside your bed, depending on what we're doing. Don't get me wrong. I'm not saying I wanna be your sub 24/7. I'm not looking for a full-time Master. I don't think I could do that."

I certainly didn't want that. "Let me see if

Damon & Pete: Playing with Fire

I've got this right." God, I hoped I had, because this was fast becoming the best day of my life in a long, long while. "You're saying you want to be my partner, sharing my life, but not losing what we have together. You're telling me you want it all—a Master *and* a lover."

Pete's breathing hitched, and a tremor rippled through him. "Yes," he whispered.

I bit my lip. "You don't want much, do ya? Anyone ever tell you what a greedy boy you are?" His eyes widened, and I couldn't torment him a moment longer. "Then I guess that makes me just as greedy, because I want it all too." I brushed my fingertips over the face I'd come to know so well. "I'd decided to ask you to move in with me. I was gonna broach the subject when we got back after the party, but then things went a little… astray." I gave him a rueful smile. "Best laid plans, huh?"

Pete was breathing a bit faster. "Move… move in with you?"

"Well, not tonight," I joked. "But yeah, when you feel you're ready for that, we can talk about it." I held my arms wide. "Come up here, boy."

In a couple of heartbeats, I had my arms full of a warm, gorgeous man who straddled me, his arms around my neck, his lips fused to mine, and they were the sweetest kisses ever. I couldn't stop touching him, stroking his back and arms, reassuring myself this was real.

When we parted, I met his gaze again. "Boy," I said softly. When I knew he was focused on me, I smiled. "Just so you know, I will always be your Master. I may turn it down a bit, but that part of me doesn't go away. So if we're doing this, you have to know that going in."

Pete nodded. "I understand... Sir."

"But no, it won't be 24/7. I don't want that either," I assured him. "Besides," I added, "we have a lot of things to discover together. I still have your list, remember?"

"List?" Pete frowned, before staring at me with wide eyes. "Oh God. *That* list."

I grinned. This was going to be so much fun. But that was for another day. I was wrung out, and the prospect of sleeping with Pete in my arms was a welcome one. "We're not talking about that now. Bed. We can talk in the morning, especially if you still intend taking the day off and spending it with me."

"That sounds great."

"Then get off me, so we can go get in bed."

Pete clambered off my lap, and waited beside the couch while I got to my feet. Once he'd bolted the door, we went into his bedroom and closed the door. There'd be much to discuss, but it would wait until morning.

I had other plans for what was left of the night.

Pete

This had to be a dream.

I was in my bed, but so was Damon, his body curved around my back, his hands warm as they rubbed my belly and chest, his breath stirring the hair on the back of my neck. We'd lain in silence for about ten minutes, and that was just fine by me. I was happy to soak it up, let it all sink in. The fact that neither of us felt the need to talk told me so much. Sleep wasn't an option right then. The lamplight flooded my room with warmth.

"I'm sorry." Damon kissed my shoulder.

"What on earth for?" I was genuinely puzzled.

"The way I spoke to you earlier. I just wanted you away from there so I could find out what was going on. And he didn't deserve to know how important you are to me, so I kept things low key."

I'd promised myself I wasn't gonna mention it, but since he'd been the one to bring it up, I grabbed hold of my courage. "Okay, I get that, but just so you know? That fucking hurt."

He stiffened against me, then relaxed. "I deserve that. I should've explained things before I asked you to go, but to be honest, seeing him there…"

I covered his hand with mine. "I guess it was a shock after all this time. I'd probably have reacted the same way." Probably. I rolled over to face him, resting my head on my arm. "Can we talk about him now?" I didn't want to push it, and if he told me it was none of my business, then fine. But I wanted to know. This was someone who'd obviously mattered to him.

Damon cupped my cheek. "There's not much to say. Whatever his reasons for coming to see me, they had two results. I finally got the answers I'd been looking for that allowed me to close the door on that chapter of my life for good. And you know what they say. When one door closes… Now I get to open a new door to a new chapter. With you."

"He hurt you," I blurted out. I'd seen it, etched on Damon's face, there in his eyes.

Damon sighed. "Only when I realized he

never loved me, not like I'd loved him. And I'm only telling you this because I don't want any secrets between us. You need to know you can ask me anything, okay?" He smiled. "You also need to know what you're letting yourself in for."

I stroked the broad, fuzzy chest I knew so well, loving how he shivered when I brushed over his nipples. "We're gonna have rules, right? For when we play?"

He nodded. "But you have to understand that sometimes the rules will bleed into our daily life. Like I said, I can't switch it off."

"I'm fine with that," I answered truthfully. If I was honest, it was what I'd always wanted. "There *is* one thing I'd like to mention… seeing as you said I can ask for anything."

He snickered. "I already know what you want, boy. You haven't exactly been subtle about it." He trailed a hand down my hip, then caressed my ass. "And we're gonna work up to that, I promise."

For a moment I was lost. Then it came to me. His hand…. Oh fuck.

I couldn't help my reaction. I shuddered, and Damon pulled me to him.

"Not now," he said gently. "That kind of conversation is for daylight hours, when we're both thinking clearly."

"And it wasn't what I was thinking about," I confessed. When he gave me an inquiring glance, I smiled. "I want what we had the night of your mom's party."

His brow furrowed. "And what was that?"

"You, making love to me." God, I wanted that so badly.

Damon's frown disappeared, and his smile

reached his eyes. "You read my mind." He pushed me firmly onto my back and rolled on top of me, his arms bracketing my head. Fuck, I loved that feeling of being pinned to the mattress by his weight, of being able to wrap my legs around him, hook my arms around his neck, and hold on to him while he rocked us both to a climax. I'd missed the intimacy of that connection. Being tied to his St. Andrew's Cross, in a sling, whatever... yeah, those were times that still sent a shiver down my spine, fulfilling a part of me I'd always known was there, but when we were like this, as lovers...

It was like there were two halves to my soul, and Damon fit them both to perfection. Yeah, I know that sounded corny as hell, but it was *my fucking truth*, and I didn't give a rat's ass who knew it.

I was his, finally, totally, *his*, and I couldn't have been happier.

Damon

I gazed down at Pete, his calves resting on my shoulders as I guided my slick cock to his hole, his hand gently pulling on his swollen dick. I pushed against the lubed ring of muscle, not enough to penetrate it. "Whose hole is this?" I asked softly, my gaze locked on his.

"Yours." His chest rose and fell, and I was aware of his scent, a musky fragrance that made my shaft like iron.

I nodded, rubbing the head over his pucker, teasing it. Pete moaned quietly, and I knew it wouldn't be long before he was ready to bust a nut. "Hold onto it as long as you can."

He rolled his eyes. "Says you who's already cum how many times today?"

I grinned. "Says the man who can change his mind and put you in chastity if he feels so inclined."

His eyes widened. "You wouldn't. Wait, what am I saying? Of course you would."

I pushed a little harder, feeling the ring give way a little. I wasn't about to tease him any longer. He'd taken my dick earlier like a champ with no lube, albeit with an already slick hole, and hadn't asked once if he could cum.

That deserved a reward.

I hooked my arms under his knees and leaned over, pushing his legs to his chest as I slid into him, taking my time, catching my breath at the exquisite sensation that never failed to stir me. When I was fully seated, I paused, our mouths inches apart. "Love you, boy."

I wasn't sure whether his long, drawn-out sigh was a result of my dick stretching him, or my declaration. I had a feeling it was even money. I kissed him, all the while leisurely stroking my cock in and out of his hole, his dick hot against my belly.

"Love you, sir," he whispered, before grabbing his knees so I could sit up and establish a rhythm, an unhurried rocking that would bring us both to where we wanted to be.

Sticky, cum-covered heaven, followed by a night of restful sleep.

The first night of many.

Take My Hand

Pete

December

"So, this is a Christmas party we're going to?" I asked as I watched myself squirm into the tight leather pants Damon had gotten me the previous week. "Are we talking garlands and Christmas trees?" I had a feeling it wasn't that kind of party.

"Hardly. It just happens to take place during the holidays. And no garlands, no trees, just lots of black vinyl, a sling, and a truckload of lube and condoms. Kind of a 'bring your own toys' deal." Damon walked up behind me and slid his arms around my waist, nuzzling my neck. "I'm gonna show off my boy."

"You're trying to distract me," I said accusingly, glaring at the mirror. Not that I minded in the slightest. Kissing me there always revved up my engine.

"Guilty. I don't want you dwelling on it right now." I shivered, and he tightened his arms around me. "You remember what I said? You can say—"

"I'm not gonna change my mind," I insisted. I'd fantasized about this for long enough, I was more than ready for the reality. "Besides, we've been working toward this for months." The long build-up, the dildos, the talking… All of it had only increased my longing. The fact that Damon had done this before eased a lot of my early anxiety, when he told me we were really going to do this.

Making me wait until December was the tortuous part.

Damon stared at my reflection in the mirror. "Sit with me for a moment."

I knew what that meant. I waited until he was on the bed, pillows supporting him, his legs spread wide for me to sit there with my back to him. I leaned against him, his arms around me, and that was so much better. This was my safe place, where both of us felt free to share whatever was on our minds.

Damon kissed my temple. "I know you can take that mammoth of a dildo, but we both know me pushing my hand inside you is *not* the same thing. It's not just something else to fuck you with."

"I know that," I said quietly. "I remember what you said. This is as connected as it gets." My own feelings had changed. When he'd first mentioned fisting me, back in the summer, all I could think of was how *fucking hot* that sounded. But now? This was more about us connecting on another level, one that required ultimate trust and intimacy. I knew he'd be watching out for me every fucking second, to make sure he didn't hurt me, and to see I got the most out of the act. I loved that it wasn't just me who wanted this: Damon couldn't wait either.

"Did you do what I said?"

I nodded. "Yes, sir." I'd spent an hour that morning, sitting quietly, mentally preparing myself. I'd pictured myself being stretched by Damon's large hand, pictured his eyes focused on me while he stilled his hand inside me. That had been enough to give me a hard on. As the day progressed, I kept a tight hold on those feelings of desire and longing.

I was glad he didn't ask me if my ass was ready for him. It was bad enough going through an enema without having to talk—or even think—about it afterward. And talking about cleaning out your ass? Number one mood killer right there.

"Ready to go?" Damon kissed my head.

I twisted my neck to stare at him. "Aren't you forgetting something?"

He chuckled. "Like you'd let me." I scrambled off the bed and hurried over to the dresser beside the mirror. Damon followed, laughing quietly. A moment later he was fastening my collar around my neck. That never failed to give me a thrill. *My* collar. It wasn't the leather one I'd worn to the Folsom party. This was more like a heavy chain with a padlock, and I loved wearing it. He always joked I was like a little kid, putting it on the minute I got home from work. He could laugh all he wanted—it was mine, bought for me, and my proof *right fucking there* that I was his. This would be the first time he was going to take me to a sex party wearing it. We hadn't been to one since Folsom, and I couldn't wait. That had been amazing.

This one promised to be off the charts.

"Better?" Damon's gaze met mine in the mirror.

"Better." Wearing his collar so all his friends knew I was his?

Totally hot.

Damon

"Is that wise? Leaving Pete alone with Ray?" Jake chuckled. "Then again, if anyone can tell him what to expect, it's Ray."

He had a point. Ray was an expert when it

came to fisting. I gazed across the room to where Ray and Pete sat on the floor in a corner, talking quietly. "In which case, we'll let them talk." All around them, the party was in full swing. RD seemed to have invited more guys than last time, and already the air was filled with the sounds of flesh smacking against flesh, paddles swooshing to connect with asses, and the grunts and groans of guys getting fucked.

I chuckled. Pete and Ray carried on talking, oblivious to it all, which made for an incongruous sight. "You'd think they were having a chat over a coffee, to look at them." I was glad Pete was making friends. I played a lot with this bunch, and I wanted him to feel comfortable.

Not that I'd played recently. Real life had intruded, but in the best way.

"We were beginning to wonder if something had happened. It's been a while since we've seen you at one of these shindigs. I think Folsom was the last." Jake grinned. "Don't think I haven't noticed his collar. Are congratulations in order?"

"Yup. And I've been busy. I never realized how much stuff I had, until Pete moved in and we had to find room for everything." It had taken us a while to get used to sharing a space—and getting used to each other's habits—but I liked the way things were moving along.

Jake gaped. "Whoa. You're living together? Wow. That's awesome."

"He put his house on the market last week. I guess that's as serious as it gets."

"Too right!" Jake chuckled. "I hope Santa is gonna bring him some very naughty presents this year."

Damon & Pete: Playing with Fire

Pete's gifts were already wrapped, hidden where he wouldn't find them. I couldn't wait to see his face when he opened them. I'd spent a whole morning at Mr. S Leather, deliberating what to get him. Then I'd said what the hell and bought a shitload of toys.

Christmas Day was gonna be a *lot* of fun.

Jake nudged me. "Tate has been watching Pete and drooling ever since you arrived. You know how much he loves blonds. And let's be honest here, he'd have tapped that cute ass in a heartbeat if you'd given him the go-ahead last time." He peered at me inquiringly.

I knew what he wanted to know. "We've... discussed playing with others." The jury was still out on that one, but judging by the number of times Pete had brought it up, he was still thinking about it positively.

"I think whatever happens, one thing is obvious. You're happy."

I couldn't help smiling. "You got that right. And so is my mom. You know what she told me when I called her to say Pete was moving in? She said she'd given up hope of me finding anyone who'd put up with me."

Jake bit his lip. "Go figure."

I glared at him. "That sounds suspiciously like you agree with her."

"Saying nothing."

Pete chose that moment to glance at me from across the room. I nodded, smiling, letting him know he was okay to keep on talking if he wanted. Because it looked like Ray was doing a great job of answering his questions.

I wouldn't let him talk *too* long, however.

His ass had an important appointment with my hand.

The hardest part about this whole event was hiding my own feelings from him. I mean, I wanted it, enough that I'd been on tenterhooks the week leading up to it. But what surprised me was that I was nervous.

I didn't get that part, not at first. I'd fisted loads of guys, from those who were experiencing their first time and wanted someone who knew what the fuck he was doing, to those who could damn near take my whole arm like it was nothing. So why the hell was I nervous?

Then it hit me.

I wasn't in love with one of those guys. I wasn't living with them. I wasn't committed to them.

This was new for me, and I wanted to experience it with Pete.

Pete

"You know what the best part is for me?" Ray asked. "When he takes his hand out."

"Really?" I tried to get my head around that. "Not when he's moving it inside you?"

Ray shook his head. "Think about when you've got a butt plug in there. When you pull it out, there's this... pop, right? Doesn't that feel good? When you're opening up those muscles from the inside?"

Now that he mentioned it... "Yeah."

"Plus, when he's got his hand in you, it's a mix of pleasure and pain. If he's any good, he'll

Damon & Pete: Playing with Fire

know how to navigate between the two."

I glanced across at Damon, who gave me a warm smile. "Oh, he's good."

Ray chuckled. "Lord, you've got it bad."

I wasn't about to deny it. I was head over heels. Three months in, and it just kept getting better.

"And another thing. You know it'll feel nothing like a plug, right? I mean, those babies are smooth, but a hand feels almost… jagged."

I snorted. "Sounds like the dragon dildo he's had me practice with this last month."

Ray's eyes widened. "Respect. Those are fucking *huge*." He snickered. "Oh, well, if you can take one of those, you might get more out of your first time than I got outta mine. It can take a couple of tries until he gets his hand in." He paused. "Don't forget poppers. They come in real handy. You take a hit right after he gets it in, and you're good to go for a while."

"What do they do?" I'd never used poppers, and I was curious.

"They give you this head rush that lasts maybe three minutes before it wears off. It gets your heart rate going, and it works wonders on your insides, relaxing the muscle. And yeah, you're kinda high for a second or two." He gazed intently at me. "You want some advice?"

"Anything." I wanted to get the most out of this.

"Remember, when you're getting fisted, you need to be out of your head and in your body, which I know sounds weird, but let me explain. When I'm getting fisted, and I'm thinking too much about what's happening and tighten up, I have a trick that really works. I get him to stop moving, just hold it real still inside me, and then I close my eyes and mentally scan through my body. I start at the top of my head, checking in with the muscles, and end at my feet. It's sorta like meditation, makes me more aware of my body, of how it feels." He grinned. "Having his hand in me? Best. Feeling. Ever. But I only do this at parties, or someplace else that's not my apartment."

"Why?"

He flushed. "Fuck, I couldn't do this at home. My neighbors would run me outta there. When I cum from being fisted? Sounds like I'm giving birth to a cow." He waggled his eyebrows. "So be prepared. Oh, and you ever see those nature documentaries about deer giving birth, and there's this little baby deer, all wobbly on its legs?" He snickered. "That'll be you, afterward. I don't know what it is about lying in a sling and having a guy's hand in you, but *fuck*, it wears you out like nothing else. I mean, like completely drained." He glanced across at Damon. "But you know what's gonna make it so much better? That connection between you. I *love* anonymous sex, but I wouldn't let a stranger fist me."

"Because you have to trust him, right? To know him, and for him to know you."

Ray nodded slowly. "Exactly. There's no high like it. And you are gonna *love* it."

That did it. I wanted Damon *right that fucking second.*

A hand touched my shoulder. "Ready to play?"

I gazed up at him. "Fuck, yeah." Before Damon could say another word, I was on my feet, thankful I'd removed the leather pants when we'd arrived. I wanted to be ready for action. And seeing so many naked guys went a long way to making me feel more at ease with being nude. I smiled to myself. It was like being at home. Neither of us spent a whole lotta time in clothes.

That's what blinds are for, right?

"Have fun." Ray gave me a grin, which I returned, before Damon took my hand and led me over to the corner where they'd set up the sling.

Showtime.

Damon

Pete trailed a hand over the sling's frame. "I remember this baby."

I glanced at his cock, already pointing up to the ceiling, and snickered. "So I see." I reached down and gave it a few leisurely strokes, noting the precum that was already beading at the slit. "I'm not surprised you took off your pants. This would've bust your zipper. Boy, you're ready to pop, aren't ya?"

He laughed. "Not yet, I'm not."

I grabbed his ass and lifted him into the sling, putting his feet in the stirrups. He gripped the chains, his eyes focused on me, and I smiled. "I know you're eager and all, but I was gonna warm you up a little first."

His eyes lit up. "With toys?"

I unzipped my leathers and fished out my rigid dick. "I was thinking more along the lines of this." I smacked it against my palm.

Pete grinned. "Like I'd ever say no to that beautiful cock."

I grabbed hold and pulled him toward me, so his ass was hanging over the edge, before slicking up my shaft and squeezing lube over his hole. A moment later I was home, all the way inside him, my hands on his thighs, pulling him toward me to meet my thrusts, Pete's hard dick bouncing against his belly. "Love the way you feel on my cock."

"Love the way... your cock feels... in my hole." He gave a blissful smile as he glanced at the sling. "Can we have... one of these... at home?"

I tried not to think about the large parcel hidden in the garage. "We'll see." A few of the guys had come over to watch us, but I shut them out. This was just me and Pete. I'd already gotten towels, lube and a couple of toys within easy reach, but I wanted him relaxed and happy.

That was a no-brainer. My boy loved to be fucked. His dick was leaking precum like a bastard all over his abs, but he knew better than to touch it. In our bed at home, making love, that was okay, but in a scene?

That sweet cock was all mine.

When he moaned with pleasure, I knew it was time. Reluctantly I pulled free of him, and grabbed a towel. "Ass up." When he complied, I slid it under him. His gaze alighted on my glistening dick, and I knew what he wanted. I stood next to his head, held my cock out, and he was on it, his hot mouth encasing my shaft. Fuck, he could suck like a goddamn vacuum cleaner, and I was way too close. "You gonna take what I give ya?"

His eyes shone, and I swear he sucked even harder. That was it. I emptied my balls down his throat, holding his head steady so he took every last drop. I shivered as he slowly licked along my dick, cleaning it with his tongue. Pete dropped his head back onto the sling mat and grinned. "Think I'm ready for my entrée."

I tucked my softened cock into my pants and reached for a thick, flexible dildo. I let him see it as I slicked it up, and he chuckled. "After that dragon cock I've been playing with? That's like fucking me with a pencil."

I laughed as I slid it into his loosened hole. "I'd agree." I pushed until three quarters of its black, glistening length was inside him, then I held up another. "Except this time, I'm fucking you with two at the same time." Patiently, I eased it into him next to the first, and he let out a soft moan. Then I set up a rhythm, sliding them alternately in and out of his ass, until his moans reached a new volume. "Like that?"

"Feels... amazing. Full. But fuck, when they *both* move..." He gripped the chains, his belly tightening as I fucked him with both.

I couldn't resist. "Imagine how it would feel if there were two dicks inside you at once."

God, his eyes widened at that. "We need... to talk about this some more." I held one still and slid the other in and out, faster and deeper, and he groaned. "Fuck, yeah, we have to talk about this."

I laughed, and gently removed them, before picking up what would be the final toy. "Got something new for ya."

He gaped. "Oh my fucking God, it looks like a traffic cone with ridges."

Not a bad description. Its head was shaped like the head of a cock, but that was where the similarity ended. It flared to a wide base that I had to stretch my hand to grasp. "It'll feel really good, and it'll open you up for me." I applied a liberal coating of lube, then pressed the head into his hole. It popped in easily, but he moaned as I twisted and turned the toy, rotating it as I slid it slowly into his ass, changing the angle now and then.

"Like those... ridges," he gasped as I drove it a little deeper.

I left it wedged in his ass, and put on my black nitrile gloves. When my fingers were slick with a heavy lube, I pulled out the cone until there were only a couple of inches inside him. This time when I slid it into him, I added a couple of fingers, and he moaned in appreciation.

"Yeah, gonna stretch you wide open, boy." Then there were three fingers inside him, and all the while I corkscrewed that cone into his hole, in and out, until his breathing grew ragged. I added a fourth finger, pushing my hand deeper into him, still moving the cone in and out until there was less of it and more of my hand inside.

I stilled my hand and checked on him. Pete's gaze was locked on mine, still gripping the chains. I smiled, gently thrusting into him maybe an inch, then stopping. "We're just gonna camp out here for a little bit," I said quietly, letting my hand slowly stretch him, feeling the muscle gradually open up for me. "Okay?"

Pete let out a rough chuckle. "Camp out. I like that." He nodded. "It's more than okay. Feels... oh fuck, it feels really good." He attempted a grin. "Better than the dragon, at any rate."

I gave him a moment to get accustomed to the stretch, knowing once I was all the way in, things would get a whole lot more serious. When I felt he was ready, I tucked in my thumb, and slowly, so slowly, eased deeper while pulling the cone free, and suddenly, I was inside him, up to the wrist.

"Oh, fuck," he groaned, his hole clamping up really fast.

I'd expected this. "Breathe, Pete. Breathe slowly, and count to ten. I'm not gonna move. Come on, count out loud for me."

Pete commenced counting, his voice quavering, and I held still, watching for the signs that his body was relaxing. And when it happened, I saw it plain as day.

"Good boy," I said, keeping my voice soothing. "We don't go any further until you're ready." I grabbed the small amber bottle and held it to his nostrils, watching him take a hit.

That's it, boy. I was so fucking proud of him.

Pete

I was aware of my heartbeat, racing a little faster. I focused on my body, like Ray had told me, and God, it was amazing how my muscles relaxed. I could feel his hand, so fucking huge inside me, and I understood why you might think a hand felt jagged. "Fuck, your knuckles…" It was a weird moment, heady sensations all mixed together with a good dose of high.

Damon nodded. "And if I move them slightly, you'll feel it."

I stared at him. "Do it." I breathed deeply, forcing myself to keep calm. The movement of his hand was so gentle, a slight thrust, no more, but fuck, I felt it. He stilled again, his eyes on me, and I knew words were useless.

We were beyond words.

Damon made his hand vibrate just a little inside me, and there I was, dancing along that line between pain and pleasure. Except... it was more discomfort than pain.

"Feel my hand?" I nodded. "Try to grip it with your butt muscles, then relax them." I did as he asked, unable to miss the moment when he felt it too. Damon smiled. "Oh wow. Yeah. Okay, keep doing that, but now visualize my hand sliding in. I'm not gonna twist it, all right? Just gonna keep it like this, a gentle in and out motion. That's all you'll need to cum from this."

I did as he suggested, getting into a rhythm of grip-relax-grip-relax, all the while picturing his hand inside me, inching its way a little deeper. I kept my breathing steady, and then it hit me than Damon's breathing was synchronized with mine, that we were locked in this moment of almost... meditation, as he gently moved inside me.

That was when I knew I was ready for more.

"Now," I whispered. Damon placed one hand on my belly, slowly rubbing it while he moved in and out of my hole, no more than an inch or two, but I felt it. I felt his knuckles when he flexed his hand a little, and fuck, that was hot. I lost all track of time, conscious of nothing but that hand inside me, and Damon's gaze locked on me. He'd pause now and again, and each time he recommenced those gentle movements inside me, I moaned from the exquisite pleasure of it all. It wasn't like I'd expected. No frenzied hand-fucking, no slipping in and out of my hole, just that unhurried, almost reverential motion as he brought me closer to the edge with one- or two-inch thrusts. I felt every single one of them. By then I was covered in sweat, my chest heaving, and I knew I was going to cum from this.

"Touch yourself," Damon said, his eyes focused on mine.

I wrapped my hand around my cock and tugged, and Damon sped up a little, never once breaking eye contact. Nonsensical words poured from me as I shot my load, giving way to a low moan that wouldn't stop, that was so fucking *loud,* I swear everyone in a five-mile radius heard it. Heat poured off me, cum pulsed out of me, and still I couldn't hold the sound in. Damon came to a rest, his face alight, and I was so fucking ecstatic to share this with him.

Then came the moment when he pulled his hand free of me. I tensed, and there it was, that awesome sensation as his knuckles popped free of my hole. I groaned, not wanting it to be over.

"I know," he said softly. He removed the gloves and dropped them, turned inside out, to the floor. Damon wiped his hands and forearms on a towel, then commenced the ritual of cleaning me up. I was barely aware of it, dazed, trembling and damp, and still on such a fucking high from the rawness of it all. I didn't think I could move, and I'd never felt so... naked. Damon removed all traces of cum and lube, lifted me from the sling, and carried me over to the vinyl-covered couch where he just held me in his arms, kissing my face, stroking my chest and belly, the movements soothing and gentle.

After a while, he cupped my chin and looked me in the eye. "You okay?"

I laughed weakly. "Fuck, I'm exhausted."

"Was it like you expected?"

"Hell no. It was way better." It was something I wanted to do again, and again.

"You were amazing."

I reached up and stroked his cheek. "You know what? I think it takes two to be amazing." Then I grinned. "Although... maybe three works just as well. Just saying."

Damon laughed triumphantly. "Aha. Someone *really* liked taking two dildos."

I narrowed my gaze. "You knew I'd like it, didn't ya?"

He shrugged. "I just don't want you to miss out on anything. I know we talked about including others, but it really is up to you."

For the first time, I saw how things could be. "We play together?"

He nodded. "Always. And the moment you're not happy, you say so and it stops." He leaned over and kissed me softly on the lips. "Other guys come and go, but there's only ever gonna be one Damon and Pete. Me and my boy. My lover."

Warmth flooded through me. "I like that," I murmured. That got me another tender kiss.

Damon peered at me inquiringly. "You said three. Is that a hard limit?"

I knew that look. "Why?"

He gave a casual shrug. "I was just wondering how many guys I could squeeze into my basement for your first gangbang, that's all." His eyes glittered, and I knew he'd seen that telltale twitch of my dick.

I laughed. "To quote you, let's not run before we can walk, okay? I think we need to work up to that one." Who was I kidding? He'd had me thinking about that when he first mentioned it back in the summer.

Damon grinned, and I knew he wasn't fooled. "Maybe. I was thinking we'd give it a couple of months. I reckon by February you'll be asking me who's coming." He snorted. "Apart from you, of course."

Life with Damon was never gonna be boring. And I intended to enjoy every minute of it.

Pete's TREAT

TANTALUS

Copyright information
This is a work of fiction. Names, characters, places, and incidents either are the product of the author's imagination or are used fictitiously, and any resemblance to actual persons, living or dead, business establishments, events, or locales is entirely coincidental.

Pete's Treat
Copyright © 2019 by K.C. Wells writing as Tantalus

Cover Art by Meredith Russell

The trademarked products mentioned in this book are the property of their respective owners, and are recognized as such.

All Rights Reserved. No part of this book may be reproduced or transmitted in any form or by any means, including electronic or mechanical, including photocopying, recording, or by any information storage and retrieval system without the written permission of the Publisher, except where permitted by law.

PETE'S TREAT

Valentine's Day is coming, and Damon was never one for saying it with flowers.
He has something a lot more… primal in mind.
Pete struggles with what to buy Damon. What do you get for the man who needs nothing?
As for Pete, he thought he had everything he wanted – until now…

Pete's Treat

The Way Things Are.

Damon

January

It had to be my favorite view. Pete, on all fours, his long, lean back stretched out, his ass in the air, and my fat dick sliding into it, splitting those cheeks and sending shudders through Pete every time I went deep.

Then I smiled to myself. *Who am I kidding?* I loved it when Pete was on his back, mouth and eyes wide as I drove my cock home. When Pete sat on my shaft, his fingers digging into my shoulders as he rolled those slim hips, his belly taut, his nipples begging to be sucked and teased and pulled on. When I pinned Pete to the bed with my weight, rocking my hips as I fucked the cum out of him, my hand clamped to Pete's mouth, muting his cries.

I loved Pete any which way I could.

I covered him with my body, nuzzling the back of his neck. "That feel good, boy?" I spread him wide with my legs, moving only my hips while I enjoyed every inch of that tight body wrapped around my shaft.

"Like you have to ask," Pete groaned. He shivered as I slowly pulled out of him, only to drive my dick all the way home with one hard thrust. "Fuck, I missed this."

I pumped into him, short, fast strokes that had him moaning almost instantly. "Yeah, right. You've got a nightstand full of toys. I bet your ass is worn out after riding that dragon dildo while I've been gone." Two nights I'd been away, for a conference, and they'd been the longest two nights ever. Not that I'd done without. The first night I'd called him from the hotel to indulge in a little late-night dirty talk.

Pete's moans as he shot his load were all I'd needed to get me off to sleep.

"Haven't... played with it... once. Was waiting for... the real thing." He arched his back, tilting his ass higher. "Oh fuck, yeah. *That* real thing, right there." I grabbed his hips, pulled him up onto his knees, and mounted him, spearing my cock deep into that hot, tight furnace, anchoring myself to his shoulders. "Yeah, oh yeah, fuck me."

Later that night, there'd be loving, and tenderness, and words whispered in the dark as I made sure Pete knew how much I loved him. Right then, a hot quick fuck was just what the doctor ordered to cure all my ills.

Two nights of no Pete in my bed, in my arms.

Two days of not seeing him, making him laugh, sharing his day.

Fuck, what happened? One minute I'd

been a self-reliant guy, not needing anyone, and the next? I needed him like he was air.

And I wouldn't go back to how I was. Not for a second.

Max poured us another coffee, then settled back into his chair. Beyond his office door, the kitchen was quiet: the lunchtime rush was over, and preparations were being made for dinner.

He'd obviously timed our meeting for coffee with precision.

"So, how's the boy toy?" Max's eyes twinkled.

I pushed out a growl. "Don't call him that. And he's twenty-nine soon. Not exactly a boy, is he?" Not that I hadn't expected this. Little brothers were supposed to be a pain in the neck, and Max was only living up to expectations.

Max snorted. "In comparison to *your* forty years, he sure is. What was wrong with finding a guy your own age?"

I put down my coffee cup. "I wasn't *looking* for a guy. He sort of snuck up on me." And wasn't *that* the truth?

"And you still haven't answered my question. How is he? Is he driving you crazy yet? Because after all these years of living alone, having someone else around the place must be a... challenge." He grinned. "To put it mildly."

"You'd be surprised." Because I certainly was. Pete had slotted into my home and my life like he'd always belonged there. Sure, there'd been disagreements in the early days, but we'd adjusted fairly quickly to a routine that suited us. Those days when my appointments finished early, I was the one to make dinner. When he worked from home, designing gardens, Pete was in charge. And as for chores, we divided them equally. The dishwasher was our friend, and the toilet our enemy, but at least we both had good aim where the latter was concerned. I liked order and neatness, and Pete was a fast learner.

And on those occasions when he wasn't, there was always my paddle…

"Mama thinks the world of him, that's for damn sure." Max chuckled. "Her face when you brought him for Thanksgiving… I don't think she stopped smiling all day. You earned yourself a shitload of points that day."

"All I did was bring him along." Pete had been nervous at first, but I'd reminded him how well Mama's birthday evening had gone. He calmed down after that.

"Yeah, but she'd just about given up on you ever bringing a boyfriend to a family gathering, and he makes it to a second one." Max scrunched up his eyebrows. "Except 'boyfriend' sounds wrong. Kinda out of place. Partner, maybe?"

I said nothing. I preferred my word. Boy. Not that I called Pete my boy all the time. That was mostly for when we were engaged in intimate pursuits. An image rose in my mind. Pete's head on a cushion on the floor, his weight on his shoulders, while I stood above him, spread his legs like a wishbone and did a pile driver number

Damon & Pete: Playing with Fire

on his hole. Me gazing down at him, feeling his body squeezing my cock, demanding to know if he was my boy.

Those eyes, locked on mine, hotter than hell as he nodded. *'Your boy. Yours.'*

Yeah. There were some things Max really didn't need to know.

"Hey, now here's a thought. Valentine's Day is coming up." Max let out a wry chuckle. "Who knows what might be waiting for you when you get home from a hard day's doing whatever it is you do." His lips twitched. "You might find him stark naked on a bed of rose petals, with a big red bow tied around his dick."

I arched my eyebrows. "Do you think a lot about stuff like that? Naked guys on beds of petals? Is there something you want to tell me?"

Max rolled his eyes. "Yeah, right. That stuff doesn't bother me. Hell, I've seen worse in those magazines you kept under your mattress." I gaped at him, and he nodded. "You think I didn't know what you were hiding under there? Fifteen years old, and I was exposed to photos of naked men fucking. Scarred me for life." He smirked. "Actually, it helped me decide one thing. I was definitely straight, because hell, they did nothing for me."

I guffawed. "Then you owe me." I helped myself to more coffee. "And it's funny you should mention Valentine's. Pete has been trying—in a not-so-subtle way—to work out what to get me for a gift. He's been talking about music, books, clothes... The thing is? I have everything I need. I certainly don't need more stuff."

"And what about *his* gift?"

I smiled. "Oh, I had that worked out weeks ago. It's all planned."

Max stared at me for a second, then his mouth fell open. "Oh. My. God."

"What?"

He shook his head. "You're gonna do it, aren't ya?"

"Do what?" He'd truly lost me.

"Propose to him. That's it, isn't it? You got the ring already?" He appeared absurdly happy about the prospect.

"Pro—" I burst out laughing. "God, no."

"It's not that hilarious a suggestion, is it?" Max frowned. "I mean, you must love him. You live together."

There was no way I was about to explain to Max that Pete's collar was as close as we got—or wanted to get—to being married. "We're both happy with things the way they are," I said quietly. "Neither of us want marriage, so why rock the boat? We don't need a piece of paper to show we're committed."

No. We had that heavy chain around Pete's neck, that told anyone who needed to know, exactly what the situation was.

Max nodded slowly. "I guess I got carried away at the idea of standing with you. You know, in a church, with Mama crying her eyes out in the row behind?"

I was touched. "Well, if we ever change our minds, I'll know who to ask." Not that there was much chance of that. Pete was perfectly content with our life.

Maybe once upon a time, I'd had that dream too, but after so many years of being alone, now that I'd found *my* corner of Happiness, I was going to make sure I didn't screw it up.

Max glanced at the clock. "Want to share some pasta before you go? Donny made this sage tortellini in a butter sauce that's to die for."

I was about to refuse, but the lure of sage and butter was too much to ignore. "Just a little. I don't want to ruin my appetite."

Besides, if I wasn't all that hungry when I got through the front door, I could always compensate by taking Pete down to the basement for an appetizer.

A good, hard fuck always made me ravenous.

Ulterior Motives

Pete

"Well? What do you think?"

I wasn't sure where to start. Okay, so it was a well-maintained yard, but there wasn't that much scope for doing something 'adventurous', which was why she'd asked me to take a look at it. "Mrs. Ramos, I—" Her heavy sigh stopped me dead in mid-sentence.

She gazed at me sadly. "When do you think you might get around to calling me Mama? After all, you're living with my son. Mrs. Ramos makes it sound like it's not... permanent."

"Oh. I was just being polite, that's all." The last thing I wanted was to offend her.

"I know you were. You're a polite young man."

"And I was going to try to work up to it, honest. It's just that Damon and I, we've only been together a relatively short time. It felt... wrong to leap right in and call you Mama." I'd assumed that was a word for when we'd gotten used to the situation. And I had no idea when that would be. It still felt like a dream to me. But I knew what she meant about the whole 'not feeling permanent' thing.

I just wasn't sure what to do about it.

She gestured to the couch by the window, and we sat. "I have a confession," she said quietly. Her manner was so unlike the feisty woman I'd come to know, that I was instantly intrigued. "I... got you here under false pretenses."

I snickered. "That's okay. I didn't really

come here to discuss your yard either."

Mrs. Ramos blinked. "You're kidding. Okay—you go first."

I settled back against the cushions. "I need your help. It's Valentine's Day soon, and I want to get Damon a gift he'll remember. The only problem is, I have no clue. I've tried being subtle, but he's just not biting. So, I figured *you* might have an idea or two."

"I guess saying it with flowers is not going to work? Or chocolate?" Her expression was hopeful.

I chuckled. "You tell me. Can *you* see Damon being impressed by flowers or chocolate?"

She bit her lip. "Maybe not." Then her eyes lit up. "What about chocolate flowers? Just kidding." Mrs. Ramos mirrored my body language and leaned back. "It was hell coming up with birthday and Christmas presents when he was a child. I always took the easy way out."

"And what was that?" My brain perked up at that. *There's an easy way?*

"Books. Never failed. Of course, *I* couldn't pick out the books. Lord, no. I had to give him a gift card and let him choose his own." She locked gazes with me. "I hate to say it, but the gift Damon values the most? Is the gift where it means something to both of you. There's something personal about it, or it has special meaning to you…" She patted my knee. "I never learned the trick. Maybe *you* can."

I'd have to think long and hard about that.

"Okay, now it's your turn. Why am I really here?" If it wasn't the yard, then I had no clue. If Mrs. Ramos wanted things doing around her home, she had plenty of kids who'd be there in a heartbeat. And apart from my green thumb, I wasn't the practical type.

She fell silent for so long that the skin on my arms erupted in a carpet of goosebumps. "I guess you hit on it with the whole 'Mrs. Ramos' thing." She sighed. "It's nothing you've done, Pete. It's just… I want to see Damon settled down."

Relief flooded through me. "I sold my house and moved in with him. How much more settled do you want him to be?"

Her eyes sparkled. "How settled? I'll tell ya. Enough to see my baby married."

Oh.

Before I could say a word, she held up her hand. "I know, I know, I'm being a typical pushy mother. Most people your age aren't getting married. They're living together, just like you two. And I know a scrap of paper and a ring wouldn't change a thing between you… it's just the way I was brought up. That if you love someone, you marry them."

Fuck. How in hell could I reply to that?

"I do love him, y'know," I said softly. "Never loved anyone the way I love Damon."

The affection in her expression was so obvious, it set off a fresh round of goosebumps. "I know, sweetie. I can see that every time you look at each other. And it doesn't really matter what an old lady thinks. It's your life, after all. I shouldn't have said anything."

I covered her hand with mine. "You carry on saying whatever you want," I said firmly. "And please, don't worry about Damon. He has everything he wants, believe me."

Mrs. Ramos snorted. "Now *that*, I can believe." She cleared her throat. "So... my yard. Any suggestions?"

"Pave it over and fill it with pots?" I grinned, knowing exactly how she'd take it. She cackled, and hit me on the arm. Then it was down to the real business of sketching out what she *could* have out there—if she really wanted to be bold.

It wasn't until I was driving away that I got to thinking. And what could I have, if I was to be bold? Because sure, Damon had everything he wanted.

Did I?

I *thought* I had.

I had Damon, in my life, 24/7. I had his collar. I was his boy.

Then I reasoned that I was only thinking this way because she'd come out and mentioned marriage. Would I have even considered the idea before that? And who said Damon even *wanted* to get married? He hadn't said a word.

Damon wasn't the kind of man to keep quiet when he wanted something. Ever.

By the time I got home, I'd pushed the thought out of my mind. Why was I even wasting time on this? We didn't need a piece of paper. We were solid.

Except the damage was done. Several times that afternoon, my attention wandered from my task of designing a Japanese garden, and there I was, questioning my feelings. Analyzing our relationship.

Wondering what the hell Damon would

say if I just came right out and asked if he'd ever thought of us getting married.

Part of me didn't want to consider how I'd feel if he stared at me incredulously, with that 'What the fuck?' look in his eyes.

I didn't think I could stand that.

Coffee and Catchup

Damon

February 5th

"It's good to see you." I had to admit, marriage certainly suited them. Brayden had put on a little weight since the wedding a year ago, but that was no bad thing. He looked happier that I could ever recall seeing him, and that was saying a lot, considering how many years we went back. Tim was as laid-back as ever, his arm around Brayden's shoulders, glancing now and again at his husband, their gazes meeting for just a second. Then it was back to the conversation.

Brayden took a drink of his latte. "I'm glad you could fit us in. I know you're busy these days." His eyes sparkled. "What's this I hear about a new man?"

I groaned. "And which little bird told you that?" It wasn't as if we moved in the same circles anymore. They had their life in Sacramento, and had been blissfully loved-up since they got married. Not to mention enjoying their fill of Sacramento's gay bars and clubs.

Tim smirked. "Well, seeing as we had dinner last night at Max's place… who do you think?"

"I *think* I'm gonna kill my brother." They laughed. "So yeah, there's someone. And I'm sure Max has told you all about him."

"Surprisingly, no. That's why we couldn't wait to meet up for coffee. We wanna hear everything." Brayden grinned. "Like, where did you meet, what's he like… and does he share the same… proclivities?"

I speared him with a look. "I keep telling you, don't go using those big words on me."

"That means yes," Brayden said with a smug air.

I'd met Brayden in college, and we'd remained friends. Our tastes did *not* run in the same vein, as I'd discovered when I took him with me to visit a certain store. Not that I'd wanted anything outrageous from Mr. S Leather—I was just checking the place out—but my God, Brayden's expression when he saw some of the 'toys'. His eyes were out on stalks.

As for me? I was in Heaven.

I sighed heavily. "Okay. Yes. Happy now?"

"I think we're more interested in knowing if *you* are," Tim said with a smile.

That was easy. "Yeah, I am. He's younger than me, but the age gap doesn't worry me. What matters most is that he *fits*, better than I ever expected any guy to do."

"Thank God for that." Brayden expelled a long breath. "If you knew how long I've waited to see that look on your face again."

"What look?"

He grinned. "The 'I'm stupid in love' face. Been a damn long time coming." Tim nudged him, and he gave a start. "Yeah. Right. Anyhow, we wanted to invite you and…."

"Pete," I supplied, smirking.

"Yeah, Pete—to our anniversary party. We're a little late in asking, because *someone* didn't get his finger out of his ass quick enough, and the venue we wanted got booked up. So we

Damon & Pete: Playing with Fire

had to arrange an alternative."

Tim rolled his eyes. "You're not gonna let me forget that, are ya?"

"Nope." Brayden's eyes twinkled with amusement.

"When's the party?" I got out my phone to check. Seeing as the only non-family parties I'd taken Pete to had been sex parties, a little slice of normality would be good. That was assuming everyone kept their clothes on.

"February 14th." Brayden took hold of Tim's hand. "We thought it would be kind of... romantic. And great for our single friends who always feel left out on Singles Awareness Day." He smirked. "AKA Valentine's Day."

"Ah." Bummer. "Sorry, guys, but we have plans for that night. Very important plans."

"Do tell. That's if you feel you can," Brayden added.

I hesitated, and he opened his eyes wide. "Aha. You have..." He leaned forward and lowered his voice. "Something kinky in mind."

Tim straightened. "Really? What?"

"It's not a big deal. I've been to hundreds of these." Then I reconsidered. "Except that's not strictly true. It *is* a big deal—to Pete. It's something he's thought about, talked about, and fantasized about, so I figured it was time for me to make it a reality."

"Now you've really intrigued me." Brayden leaned forward again. "What is it?" he whispered.

I took a deep breath. "A gangbang. I've invited three friends to come over. We've spent the last week exchanging emails, sharing our latest

test results."

Tim coughed, hastily mopping up coffee. "You're giving him a gangbang... for Valentine's Day?" He gave a furtive look around the coffee shop, as if checking that no one was listening in to our conversation.

"You don't think he'll appreciate the thought?" For the first time, I wavered. Had I got this all wrong?

Brayden guffawed. "Oh sure. I mean, nothing says 'I love you' like 'Come in here where I have three friends waiting to fuck you bareback'."

Before I could react, Tim regarded Brayden with a plaintive expression. "Oooh... can I have one of those for my birthday?" Then he jerked his head toward me. "A raw gangbang?"

I nodded. "They're on PrEP, and have all undergone testing to make sure they don't have so much as a fungal nail infection. And Pete and I haven't used condoms since Christmas. I got our latest clean bill of health two days ago."

Brayden regarded me closely. "You've obviously put a good deal of thought into this, if you're vetting everyone."

"Oh yeah. I know he wants this. And I want him to be happy." That brief flare of panic had subsided. We'd discussed his limits enough times, and I'd hinted at bringing in more guys after his fisting. If he hadn't mentioned it again after that, I'd have let it drop.

Only, he did. More than once. That was what had convinced me I was on the right track, in the end.

I was going to blow his mind.

"I suppose video would be out of the question," Tim said innocently. When Brayden gasped, he shrugged. "What? I think it sounds phenomenally hot. Totally jealous here."

Brayden aimed an accusatory glance in my direction. "*Now* look what you've started." Then he started laughing. "Well, this has been a most educational coffee break."

"Educational?" I frowned.

He snickered. "Oh yes. I'm only now discovering what a kinky guy I married. He's managed to keep this quiet for years, but the cat is well and truly out of the bag." He took Tim's hand.

"Think of all the fun you'll have." I grinned. "So many things to see and do."

"I was thinking Folsom might be a good place to start," Tim said in a matter-of-fact tone. When both Brayden and I gaped at him, he frowned. "What?"

"Don't run before you can walk," I advised him. Tim reminded me of Pete.

In which case, Brayden was going to have his hands full. One look at his smirk, and I couldn't resist. "And I don't know what *you're* looking so pleased about. You've got some catching up to do, because apparently, vanilla isn't going to cut it anymore."

That wiped the smug expression from his face. Not that I was thinking about what lay in store for them.

I was already anticipating Valentine's Day.

The Day

Pete

February 14th

Damon took one look at me and shook his head. "I swear, you're vibrating."

"I'm buzzing! I've been like this ever since breakfast. And, can I just say, that was *mean*. Telling me this morning that I had a surprise coming, but I'd have to wait for it until the evening?" I hadn't stopped thinking about it all day. Wondering. Fantasizing.

I was a mess. Work? Forget work. I couldn't concentrate for long enough. There wasn't just my surprise to contemplate. There was also the one I had planned for Damon.

The one that was giving me heart palpitations.

"I wanted to build your excitement." Damon grinned. "Did it work?"

I aimed a look at him that hopefully promised retribution when the day was over. "Can't you give me a hint?"

Damon stroked his chin, then smiled. "Yes. You'll love it."

I resisted the urge to whine. "Something a little more concrete than that?" He peered up toward the ceiling, and I let out a growl. "I'm pretty sure the answer's not up there."

"Okay," he said slowly, appearing to relent. He left me and walked into our bedroom, returning with—

An enema kit. Hoo boy.

Well, that told me one thing. Whatever

was happening, my ass was in for a surprise. And just like that, a switch flipped.

Whatever was happening was new. I felt it, from balls to bones.

"When do you want me ready?" I kept my voice low and even, doing my best to control the excitement bubbling inside me.

Damon's eyes shone with approval. "Eight o'clock. There's soup for dinner. Once we've eaten, you're to go prepare yourself."

"And… how do you want me? I mean, is there anything you'd like me to wear?"

Another warm, approving glance. "Just that jock I bought for you. The one you wore for the Folsom after-party." He grinned. "The one that barely contains your cock."

This was getting better and better. "Are we… going somewhere?"

"Yes, but not far." His lips twitched. "Just make sure you're ready for eight." Then he leaned over and kissed me. "I'm gonna make it a Valentine's Day to remember." He paused, and I knew exactly what was going through his mind. He'd gotten the cute card from me that morning, a red background with two guys' heads silhouetted against it, with a pair of hearts and a thought bubble containing the words, 'I can't even think straight.' And I knew he was looking around, waiting for his gift.

That didn't materialize.

Well, if he could tease *me*….

"I have a surprise for you too," I said quietly. "But that's for later."

He laughed. "I see. Then I guess I'll have to wait too. Do I need to clean out my ass for *your* surprise?" he said jokingly.

I couldn't waste an opening like that. I leaned in close, until our lips were almost touching, then whispered, "Only if you're gonna let me fuck you again."

Damon's breathing hitched. He wound his fingers through my hair, and held on tight as he kissed me, with none of the tenderness of before. This was a brutal, fierce claiming, and I fucking loved it. When he released me, I chuckled.

"See? I knew you loved it."

It was all bluff, and we both knew it. Topping Damon when he was tied up was one thing. I'd done it to make sure he knew I wasn't going anywhere, and that I wanted him. Now that I had him? I had no inclination to repeat the experience.

Except if he asked me to.

Damon reached down and squeezed my butt cheeks. "Just make sure you're so squeaky clean, I could use your ass as my dinner plate. And you might wanna put in a butt plug once you're done." His gaze met mine, and he grinned. "Well, you said you wanted hints. But that's all you're getting."

Whatever he had planned, one thing was obvious.

My ass was in for an unforgettable evening.

"Ready?"

I opened the bedroom door and stood there in my boots and a leather jock, my collar around my neck as usual. I did my best not to tremble, but fuck, I was nervous. He'd instructed me not to come out of our room for the last half hour.

Damon looked me up and down, nodding. "Perfect." He fingered the collar and smiled. "My boy."

"Yours," I whispered. I took advantage of his perusal to take in what he was wearing. Damon with a black leather harness snug across his chest was a magnificent sight, but my attention was drawn to the leather shorts that were barely more than briefs, his dick straining the pouch. My fingers itched to touch that solid length, but I knew better. I kept my hands to my sides and waited as he crossed the room, went to the dresser, opened a drawer, then returned to me, something black and soft in his hands.

"You'll wear this at first," he said as he tied the blindfold at the back of my head.

At first came as a relief. So at *some* point this evening I'd get to see what was going on. "Yes, sir. Will…. Will I need a coat or something to cover me?" I had visions of him leading me out to the car, all the neighbors gawking at me.

"I thought you liked the idea of exhibitionism," Damon said with a snicker. "And the answer is no. Now, here's my arm. I'm going to lead you through the house."

"Wait. There's a bag on the bed. It's got a towel and stuff in it. You know, after care." My heart hammered. I had to take that bag.

A moment later, Damon said. "Okay. I've got it. Though I'm pretty sure I can take care of all that."

I took his arm and walked slowly and carefully toward the rear of the house, but rather than head for the back door, Damon took a turn. Mentally, I tried to envisage our surroundings.

We were at the door to the basement.

Relief flooded through me. "You weren't kidding when you said we weren't going far."

Damon laughed, close beside me. "Okay, you know what the stairs look like. Put your hand to the wall as you go down."

I obeyed, feeling my way down the stairs into the cooler temperature of the basement. Except… it was warmer down there than usual. I could feel it. When I reached the bottom, I stood still, unsure of what was around me. Damon took my hand and guided me further into the space.

"Very nice, Damon." The voice was deep and gruff—and familiar. I froze, frantically replaying that voice in my head. Tate. The guy who'd fingered my ass while I'd been on my knees, sucking Damon's cock in the middle of Folsom Street.

Oh fuck. He's organized a threeway.

Damon had hinted at it often enough, and I'd thought about it ever since he first brought up the idea. And now that it was really going to happen?

I was surprised I didn't come on the spot.

"Fuck, look at that dick. He's already like a rock."

Okay, that wasn't Tate. That was…. An image came to mind. A bear of a guy, so similar to Damon in build, with big hands. Come to think of it, one of those hands was usually deep inside Ray's rectum. *That's Jake. Okay,* not *a threeway then.*

Well, Damon *had* asked me if three guys

was a hard limit.

"Oh, this is going to be so much fun."

Who the hell is that?

I stood still, rooted to the spot. Warm air brushed my neck, and I shuddered. "That's it. That's all of them." Damon's voice, low and comforting. Then his chuckle tickled my ear. "Well, I did wonder how many we could squeeze into here."

Holy fuck. His words. The Christmas party. How many guys he could squeeze into his basement for...

My first gangbang.

I swallowed, then went with humor. "Aw, for me? You shouldn't have." Laughter erupted around us.

Damon's lips met mine. Like I didn't know *his* kiss.

"On your knees, boy."

Well, Fuck Me.

Pete

I lowered myself to the floor, which was covered in some kind of fabric, not the vinyl tiles I remembered. My arms were still at my sides, my back straight. This might be my surprise, but there was no way I would let Damon down.

I'd show them his boy knew how to behave.

"Things to share before we start." Damon's voice. "I know these guys. I trust them. And we've all seen each other's paperwork. We've all been tested recently. Full medical check."

Before I could react, Damon surged ahead.

"And the reason for sharing this? No condoms here tonight, boy."

Whoa. It was exhilarating that he'd organized a gangbang for me, but a *bareback* gangbang?

Damon didn't do things by halves, and I was one lucky boy.

"Two of these guys are on PrEP. The other is HIV positive, but he's on meds and is undetectable. None of them have little nasties lurking anywhere." Fingers stroked my hair. "So by the end of this, you will be wearing their cum, or pushing it out of your hole." His breath tickled my ear. "Not to mention eating it."

Fuck.

"Your thoughts, please."

He expects me to think after delivering

that?

I swallowed. "You must think I'm safe to let this go ahead. I trust you, sir."

"Good boy." His tone was warm, and I knew I'd said the right thing.

"Ever had someone breed your ass, boy?" That unknown voice.

"Only Damon, sir." And that was new enough that it still gave me a thrill to feel his cock throb inside me.

"Can we stop jawing now?" Tate complained. "Because I for one want that sweet mouth wrapped around my cock."

Damon's hand hadn't moved from my head. "Now's the time to back out, if you want to. Your safeword is red, remember."

Like I was going to back out now.

I held my head high. "Where's that dick?"

Damon laughed. He shoved my head back and kissed me, hard and long. Then he let go. "You can get him warmed up, Tate."

Without warning, a warm cock pushed against my lips, demanding entrance, and suddenly my mouth was full of hard dick. Tate's hands cupped the back of my head as he pumped into me, my nostrils filled with the smell of leather. The sound of quickened breathing increased on all sides, and I knew they stood around me. The slap of dick against palm told me what was coming.

Fucking bring it on. Sucking cock had to be my favorite.

Music started up, a good steady beat with a rhythm that got my pulse racing. *He's thought of everything.* Above it, Tate's groan filled my ears.

"Fuck, Damon. It looked amazing... when he was sucking you off at Folsom... The reality is even better that I thought." A warm, calloused hand caressed my cheek. "Beautiful, Pete. Just beautiful."

My chest swelled, and I sucked all the harder, pulling another heartfelt groan from him.

"Enough of that. My turn." That unknown voice. Before I could ask whose dick I had the pleasure of sucking, my mouth was taken in a fierce kiss, and I responded eagerly. Seconds later, I was swallowing another hot meaty cock, only now, one of them slapped their dick against my neck. I bobbed furiously, taking in as much as I could, thankful as ever for no gag reflex.

I had but to turn my head a little to encounter fresh dick, and that was it, the pattern was set. I took it in turns to move from cock to cock, sucking along thick shafts, taking one to the root, before my hair was roughly pulled and I was filled with another. Wet sounds accompanied my endeavors, and I knew the four men were sharing kisses, while palming slick shafts, awaiting their turn. I could feel the heat from their bodies as they pressed in around me, murmuring words of encouragement.

"That's it, take it. Take that dick."

"All the way in, boy. Swallow it."

One hand on my throat. "Fuck, feel it when he takes it deep."

"You're a born cocksucker, aren't ya?"

My mouth was full of dick while another slapped me in the face.

"Make him take two." That was Tate. And then there were two cock heads pushing at my mouth, while I licked and sucked first one, then the other. "Both of 'em," Tate growled, and my lips were stretched as two hard, smooth heads fought to gain entrance.

"Gimme that mouth." That was Damon, and I was robbed of breath when he claimed my mouth in a wet, long kiss, before another mouth claimed possession.

"Time to let him see what he's playing with," said the unknown guy, and I blinked as the blindfold was pulled from my eyes. The speaker wore a pair of pale worn jeans and a harness, and I recognized him. RD, the guy whose party we'd attended after Folsom. His fly was open to reveal a long, thick shaft and full-looking balls, resting against the denim. What I couldn't miss was the heavy ring through the end of his cock. Snug around the root and balls was a black cock ring. Next to him on my right was Jake, who was naked from the waist down, apart from a pair of boots, and who wore a black vinyl shirt, the flaps open. To my left was Tate, wearing a pair of backless shorts and a snug leather vest. Two more cock rings in evidence.

Damon stood to my left, gazing at me and grinning. "Having fun yet?"

Then they turned up the heat, and my mouth was never empty.

RD held my head firm while Tate thrust into my mouth, until his dick was bumping the back of my throat. Then it was Tate holding Damon's cock steady while Jake pushed me to take it deeper. All change. Jake smacked his dick against my tongue, before Damon put both hands around my throat, his thumbs on my cheeks as

Jake fucked my mouth, until long strings of saliva fell from his glistening shaft as he pulled it free.

My own cock ached, and I yearned to take it out. "Please," I gasped out between dicks, rubbing my crotch.

Tate reached down to unzip the pouch. "Play with it," he commanded.

Like I needed to be told a second time. I curled my fingers around my hot shaft and rocked, forcing it through the tunnel of my palm. Jake trickled lube over my fingers, and fuck, that was heaven.

They towered above me, their arms around one another's shoulders as I moved from dick to dick, accompanied by the constant entreaties that fell from their lips, to *suck it, lick it, take it deep, take that fucking cock…*

It was glorious. The kisses were sloppy and fucking *perfect*, all tongues and teeth. And just when I thought it couldn't get any better, they all stopped as if by some silent agreement. RD pointed to the right. "On there, hands and knees."

There turned out to be a low bench.

Finally, I was about to get a dick in my ass. Several dicks. My hole tightened at the thought.

I got up, my knees aching slightly, and hurried to get up onto the padded surface. Tate was at my head in an instant, proffering his cock, and I took him into my mouth. The others were behind me, out of my line of sight.

Tate stroked my hair as I rocked back and forth on his girth, keeping up a constant litany of how *fucking good* it felt, and how he was going to feed me his hot load.

"Oh, nice. Look at this." Jake's tone held appreciation. Seconds later, I groaned around Tate's dick as someone pulled on my butt plug, before my body sucked it back into my hole. Then the plug was gone, and a slick cock pressed against the loosened ring. "Fuck, this is going to feel so good," Jake moaned.

"Here." Tate shoved a small brown bottle under my nose, and I helped myself to a hit. It didn't take long to feel the effects, and I shuddered as Jake drove his bare dick into me without preamble. Not that I could say a word, as another bare cock filled my mouth. Stuffed at both ends by raw dick. That was a first right there. Then all such thoughts vanished as Jake proceeded to fuck me, slamming his body against my ass.

"Oh my God, the way it fucking slides right in." He grabbed hold of my jock and held on as he thrust into me, while Tate held onto my head and pumped his dick down my throat. They got into a rhythm, aided by the thump of the music, and I rocked between them, loving the sensations.

Damon knelt beside me, his hand on my shaft, stroking it gently, working it. "That feel good?" His eyes were focused on me.

I couldn't reply. My mouth was full. Instead I moaned enthusiastically, and tried to nod my head. Damon grinned. "Me next." He got to his feet, pumping his meaty dick.

"Oh no you don't," RD called out. One moment I was full to the hilt with Jake's cock, the next, RD was plowing into me, his fingers digging into my hips. "Oh my fucking God. You get to fuck this ass all the time? When did you sell your soul, Damon? Boy's got a hole that was made to be fucked." He drove his shaft all the way home, and I cried out with sheer fucking joy. *Oh my fucking God, that Prince Albert...* It was like being rubbed on the inside in just the right way.

Jake was at my head, gently pushing Tate aside before he brushed his dick against my lips. "Wanna taste of your ass?" Then he pushed deep, and there were no more cries as I was filled again and again.

"Say you want it harder," RD demanded, thrusting into me.

"Harder, sir," I gasped out, as Jake freed my mouth.

"Didn't quite catch that."

"*Harder, sir*!" Then his hands were on my shoulders, and he was yanking me back onto that thick cock, over and over, as Jake bent down to kiss me, his tongue doing deep, while the music pumped through the air, the floor, our bodies, pushing us on with a relentless pulse.

One cock began to blur into another, as they all took turns impaling me. I moaned when Damon sank all the way into me, his hands on my waist as he filled me with his meaty shaft. "That's it, boy. Fuck yourself on my cock."

I pushed back hard, rocking onto it, loving the way he slid into me in one long glide, before spearing me with a series of short, quick thrusts. When he stopped, I moaned in frustration, until a hot tongue lapped over my hole. "Oh, fuck, yeah." I straddled the bench, spreading my legs as wide as I could, thankful for the respite.

"You like that?" RD asked. "Tate's tongue in your ass?"

Damon chuckled. "That's one thing you'll never hear—Pete complaining about getting rimmed. He'd have me eat his ass all day if he could."

I didn't laugh. I was too busy relishing Tate's talented tongue. "That feels… amazing." Hands spread my cheeks, giving him more access.

"You should see it from our viewpoint," Jake said with a snicker. "Tate on his back, his face pressed into your crack, Damon spreading you, stretching you wide for Tate's tongue…"

"Ready for my cock again," RD announced. "Tate, you stay put."

Seconds later I arched my back and groaned as RD thrust into me, slick and hot. I could still feel Tate's tongue, lapping over my balls and taint. That wasn't all he was doing.

"Fuck, yeah, that's it. Lick my shaft before I stick it inside him," RD moaned. "God, yeah, keep doing that." The dual assault on my sac and hole felt exquisite.

Damon was at my side, gripping the back of my neck as Jake thrust his cock into my mouth, all the way to the root.

The combination of sounds, smells and sensations was too much. I knew I wasn't that far from coming. When Jake pulled free of me, I shuddered out one word. "Close!"

To my horror, everything stopped, and the men stepped away from me.

Damon helped me to my feet. "Oh no. You're not to cum. We're not done with you yet. We haven't even gotten to the finale."

I gaped at him.
There's a finale?

Finale

Damon

I lay on my back on the bench, holding my dick around the base. "Climb aboard," I said with a grin. Tate threw me the bottle of lube, and I applied a liberal coating. Pete gazed down at me, obviously perplexed. "You'll find all the answers you seek when you sit on this cock," I assured him, trying to keep my face straight. God, that was corny.

Pete apparently felt the same way. He laughed and straddled me, reaching back to guide me into his hole. He sank down with a satisfied groan, until I was balls deep inside him. No sooner was my dick buried to the hilt, than I began fucking up into him, loving the shudders that coursed through him, the way he grabbed hold of my pecs and squeezed.

"That's it. You love riding this dick, don't you?"

The look on his face was answer enough. "I can never get tired… of this dick…" He leaned back, his hands on my thighs, shuddering as I drove into him.

Too far away.

"Come here," I said softly, pausing, and Pete bent over to kiss me, his hands on my face, my neck, my chest. Then he sat upright, rocking back and forth, his own cock rigid and pointing up into the air, slick with pre-cum.

I gave Jake the nod, and he stepped forward to pour yet more lube down Pete's crease, making sure it coated my shaft too. Pete rolled his hips, his eyes closed, looking as gorgeous as he always did when he let go and just... *felt*. RD straddled my head and held out his cock.

"Eyes open, boy, and take what I give you."

Pete obeyed instantly, his head bobbing as he worshiped RD's cock, appreciative noises falling from his lips. He licked around the piercing, flicking it with his tongue, and RD's groans echoed around the basement.

I met Tate's gaze, and he nodded, stepping between my legs. I grabbed onto Pete's waist. "Get ready," I ground out, stilling as I waited for Tate to get into position.

Pete pulled free of RD's dick and stared at me. "Ready for—*Jesus fucking Christ!*" He hunched over, his eyes huge, and Jake was there with the bottle again, holding it out for Pete. He took a hit from it, then shivered. "Oh fuck. Two dicks."

I reached up and caressed his cheek. "You said you wanted to try it. I didn't forget." Fuck, the effort it took not to move, but I lay there, letting Tate do all the work as he slowly pushed into Pete's body, Tate's dick sliding against mine. "You okay?"

God, his eyes were enormous. "Feels... full. God, it's..."

"Breathe. And as soon as you give the word, he's out. Okay?"

Pete drew in a deep breath. "Tate?"

Tate's hand was on Pete's shoulder, rubbing gently. "Yeah?"

"You can move now."

Tate grinned at me over Pete's shoulder. "Have I mentioned, I really like this boy?" Then he started to move, leisurely at first, a gentle rolling of his hips, but each slight thrust forced a groan from Pete's lips. "You still okay?"

Pete nodded.

Like that would be enough for me. "Words, Pete. Tell me how it feels."

His face was inches from mine. "Oh fuck. The feeling is... huge... and I don't just mean the dicks." He shuddered again. "It's like... being caught up... in some giant wave... one minute it's so fucking good... the next..." His eyes never left mine. "Don't think it'll be much longer now." He gazed down at me and mouthed, *I love you. Thank you.*

That nearly undid me right there. "I think you just gave me my gift, boy," I said softly, stroking his cheek. Pete closed his eyes, and I knew he was focusing on the sensations. "Does it feel good, having two dicks inside you?"

"Feels... stretched. Like they shouldn't fit." Pete panted. "Oh fuck, but they feel so good." Then his face tightened, and I knew he'd reached his limit.

"Not so good now? Want to stop?"

"Yes, sir."

Tate eased out of him, and Pete stood, my dick sliding out of his hot hole. I got to my feet, helped him onto his back on the bench, then grinned at the others. "Time for Pete to wear his new coat of cum."

They laughed, and soon there were four of us, pumping our dicks, standing over him while he jerked his own cock faster and faster.

RD signaled to Jake. "Grab his ankles." Jake did as instructed, and RD pushed down with his hands on Pete's thighs, before driving his cock into Pete's body. "Gotta love a hot, slick hole," he said with a groan.

"That's one long dick." Pete rolled his eyes back. "Fuck, you're deep."

RD grinned. "Which is where my load is going. Any... second... now." He froze, his thighs shaking as he cried out. Then he pulled out, wiping the last drops of cum over Pete's taint. He straightened, slowly pumping his cock. "Let's see if I can find you a bit more."

"Sounds a bit ambitious, if you ask me," Jake said with a cackle.

Pete's gaze met mine. "Come inside me, sir?"

Like I could refuse that. I lifted his legs onto my shoulders, rolling his ass up off the bench, and slid home. Pete moaned with pleasure, his hand a blur on his dick, and the others sped up their movements. It was a race to the finish as to who would be the first to shoot their load.

Jake groaned as his cum spattered across Pete's face and neck. He shook as he squeezed out the last drop. RD scooped some up with his fingers and fed it to Pete, thrusting them between his lips.

Tate was next, his body jolting as ropes of creamy white decorated Pete's abs. The last drops he saved for Pete's mouth, coating his lips with them. Then he dragged his fingers through the cum and held them out to Pete, who cleaned them with his tongue.

RD stood beside me, his breathing rapid as

he worked his shaft. "I'm not done yet."

When he stiffened, I pulled nearly all the way out of Pete. "There. Cover my cock with it."

RD moaned as drops of cum landed on my dick and Pete's sac, and I slid into Pete with ease, balls tingling as my own orgasm hit. I thrust deep into him, stilling as my cock throbbed inside him, filling him with my load.

Pete squeezed his shaft, cum pulsing out of him, filling his navel and pooling beneath the head of his dick. He closed his eyes and lay there, the odd tremor rippling through him as the remnants of his climax ebbed away.

I eased out of him, my dick still half-hard and glistening. "Now, boy. Show me that cum."

Pete grabbed hold of his legs, displaying his hole, from which a clear fluid pulsed out of him in a slow trickle. I gently pushed my middle finger inside him, releasing another rush of cum, his hole red and gaping before it shrank back to a tight pucker. "Beautiful," I said in a whisper, before scooping up the remnants and feeding it to Pete. "Here, boy."

Pete licked my fingers cleaned, sucking on them, his gaze locked on mine. Then he let go of his legs, his eyes closing, a soft sigh escaping him.

I laughed. "I think, gentlemen, we've fucked all the words right out of the boy." The others chuckled. When Pete opened his eyes, I grinned. "Got nothing to say?"

Pete slowly sat up, glancing down at his cum-covered torso and wiping his face free of its traces. "Only one thing, really." He lifted his chin and looked me in the eye. "Marry me?"

The world just... stopped.

I stared at him, my mind a blank. *He asked me… to marry him.*

Jake broke the awkward silence first. "I get it. It's a joke, right? There was that porn studio recently, where they were filming a group scene. And at the end of it, one of the guys proposed. Remember?"

Pete smiled and reached for his bag that I'd deposited on the floor.

"It's not a joke," I whispered, as Pete removed a small black velvet box from beneath his towel. I watched, transfixed, as he got up from the bench, came over to where I stood, and knelt before me.

"No, it's not." Pete didn't break eye contact. "I know we've only been together a short while, but… well… when you know, you know. I'm your boy, and nothing will ever change that… but it suddenly occurred to me that, while that may be enough for you… it's not for me. And the more I thought about it, the more I realized that *this* is what I want. To be your husband. For you to be mine. And fuck, this is the scariest thing I've ever done, because you could just look me in the eye and say—"

"Yes," I said simply.

"See? That's what I was—what did you say?"

"I said yes." I tilted my head to one side. "Did all that cum affect your hearing?" I smirked.

"But… you never mentioned wanting to get married." Pete was still staring at me.

"You never asked me." I said with a shrug. "And I never mentioned it before because I thought you were perfectly content with our life the way it was. Well... obviously you're not, so we have to do something about that. And if this is what you want... then this is what we'll do." It all made perfect sense to me.

"But not if it's something *you* don't want," Pete protested. "You can't just go along with it because it's what *I* want. We *both* have to want this."

I was conscious of the guys, watching us, so quiet.

I took a breath, and bared my soul. "There was a time, yes, when I wanted to get married. I really did. But... it was not to be. And I decided the best way not to screw anything up was... not to talk about it."

"Forgive me if I sound like a mindless idiot," Jake said suddenly. "But if *Pete* wants this, and deep down, it seems like *you* really want this too... then what is the problem? He asked, you said yes... you're getting hitched. End of."

Pete blinked. "When you put it like that..." A moment later, I had my arms full of cum-covered male. "I love you," he said quietly.

I kissed him on the lips. "I love you too. But now I think we all need to go upstairs and get cleaned up."

"Don't you want to see your engagement ring?" RD asked with a frown. Pete snickered.

Fair point. "Yes, please."

Pete opened the box to reveal a chunky yellow gold band, simple and elegant. "Do you like it?"

How could I not? It was perfect for me. "I love it." Then I chuckled. "But I am *not* putting it on until after we've had a shower."

"I suppose a group shower is out of the question," Tate asked innocently.

I pointed toward the yard. "If you three want to go have a cold shower, you're more than welcome to use the one outside by the back porch. I prefer a hot shower myself." I followed Pete to the stairs.

"We're coming too!" Tate called out.

I smiled as Pete climbed the stairs in front of me, that tight bare ass jiggling. "Fine," I yelled back. "You get the bathroom after *we're* done with it."

And as for what my boy—*fiancé*—and I might get up to in the shower, that was no one's business but ours.

Keeping Everyone Happy

Damon

May

"I've never seen you in a suit," I mused, staring at Pete's reflection in the full-length mirror.

He paused in mid-adjustment of his tie and met my gaze, his eyes bright. "Liar. You saw me in *this* suit, the day we went to try them on. In fact, you saw me in several suits." He went back to getting his tie knotted perfectly.

"Yes, but that wasn't the same thing."

Pete turned around and walked over to where I sat on the bed. "I know what you mean," he said quietly. "Now it feels... real." He glanced down. "Will I do?"

"I think you look amazing." When he reached up to touch the tie yet again, I knew there was a problem. "What's the matter?"

For a moment he said nothing. Then he sighed. "Look, I'm glad we're having two celebrations. One for your family and our friends, and another at the Eagle, but... it feels weird not to be wearing my collar. I know I'll be wearing it tonight. And I *know* I don't wear it every day, but—"

"But you wanted to wear it today."

He nodded, and the light went out of his eyes. "It's important to me."

I got to my feet, reached into the pocket of my jacket, and brought out a tied leather pouch. "Here. Mom was on at me last week, asking if I had something old, something new... *You* know. Well, I got this as the something new part." I handed it to him.

Pete's nimble fingers made short work of the knotted thread, and he opened it, removing the brown braided cord, both its ends covered in a copper-colored metal that snapped together.

"It's magnetic, so it's easily removed. But it's slim enough to be worn under your shirt. And if anyone does see it, it passes as a nice piece of jewelry." I undid his tie, popped the top buttons on his shirt, and looped the braid around his neck, clicking the ends together at the front. The cord nestled snugly against the base of his neck.

Pete touched it, before hurrying back to the mirror. "Leather," he said with a smile. "Nice touch. Thank you."

I stepped up behind him and admired the view. "Now fasten your shirt and tie, and you'll be ready." I smirked. "We can't be late for our own wedding."

Pete gave me an inquiring glance in the mirror. "What about the rest of it? Where's the something old?"

I grinned. "You're marrying it. We're going to the venue in RD's car, so that's the borrowed bit covered. And as for the blue, you'll have to wait until tonight." That was my idea of a joke. I intended putting him in chastity, then pointing out that *hey, there ya go, blue balls.* I quickly discounted that idea. That kind of joke might not go down so well on our wedding night.

Who gave a fuck about a stupid rhyme anyway?

Pete gave the tie one final tweak, then

turned around. "Done. Out of sight, but I know it's there."

"Does that feel better?" Like I didn't already know. His eyes shone, and there was a glow to him that had been missing before.

"Much."

A light tap at the door was followed by Max's loud voice. "Come *on*. You must be ready by now. Save the shenanigans for later."

"Shenan—" Pete huffed. "As if we'd be fucking *now*."

I coughed. "Before you get all self-righteous and indignant, may I remind you *why* we got up so late this morning?"

It was Pete's turn to cough.

"Guys," Max whined. "If I get you there late, it won't be *you* Mom kills."

I helped Pete into his jacket, before kissing him on the lips. "Ready?"

"Ready." He grinned. "Time for me to marry this old man."

His yelp as my hand connected with his ass was very satisfying.

Pete

The best advice for the day came from Mama. It had taken me three months, but I could finally call her that without feeling uncomfortable. I guess marrying her son made it as permanent as it could get.

Her advice was to take a mental step back

and let it all sink in.

We couldn't have picked a better day. The sun was shining, the sky was a gorgeous shade of blue, and the temperature was a pleasant sixty-two. We were standing in the Shakespeare Garden in Golden Gate Park, at the end of the long aisle where the sundial sat, a canopy of trees lining the way. Fifty or so guests sat on white chairs on the lawn, and beyond them was the terracotta facade where a table had been set up for the register.

Mama was on the front row, and with her sat Damon's siblings. Actually, Damon's family took up most of the seats, but that was fine: I had no family of my own, but I was about to become an official part of his.

On the other side sat our friends, gay men for the most part, looking extremely elegant. Damon's colleagues were there too, and I looked forward to speaking with them at the reception.

Speakers had been set up, and soft piano music filled the air. Everything fitted together perfectly, and—

Someone cleared their throat.

Two someones—the officiant, and Damon, who was staring at me, amusement in those dark eyes. "Can I put the ring on now?"

I held out my left hand, and he slid the ring into position. "I think we need to work on your concentration," he murmured.

The officiant cleared his throat again. "You have both declared your love for each other. You have both committed your lives to each other." He smiled. "You may kiss your husband."

"With pleasure," we both murmured, before laughing, our guests joining in, applauding.

Damon & Pete: Playing with Fire

Damon put his arms around me, pulling me into him, and our lips met in a lingering kiss, like we had all the time in the world.

"Get a room!" someone yelled, amid more laughter as the applause ebbed away.

"Get a bucket of cold water!" That was Max, and without looking, I knew that Mama was the cause of the loud "Ouch!" that followed. More laughter, this time at Max's expense.

I didn't care. I was lost in a kiss.

When we finally parted, the officiant gently guided us to turn to face our guests, and the applause began again, swelling to a crescendo as we joined hands and walked into the midst of our family and friends. Mama was wiping her eyes with one hand, and throwing rice with the other. People came up to us and hugged us, or patted us on the back, and from the rear, servers appeared with trays bearing glasses of champagne.

I don't know how long we chatted with our guests. It was a wonderful bubble of time. Eventually Max did his best man thing, and informed everyone that it was time to move on to the reception, which was taking place in a hotel not far from the park.

"All he needs is a dog, and he could herd them towards the exit," I muttered.

Damon snorted. "Apt image." He let out a happy sigh. "That went well."

"And we still have tonight to look forward to," I reminded him.

Tate appeared at my side, grinning. "I'm looking forward to the party at the Eagle. Of course, you *know* what we're all wondering."

Damon arched his eyebrows. "No, but I'm

sure you'll enlighten us."

"Well, it's not so much a case of wanting to kiss the bride, more like…" Tate leered. "Do we get to bang the bridegroom?"

Damon chuckled. "I guess that will be up to Pete."

I snorted. "And *I* guess that would depend on which bridegroom was getting banged. Seeing as there are two of us." I smiled sweetly. "Aren't you going to answer Tate's question?" As if I didn't know what his response would be.

Before either Damon or Tate could reply, I leaned in and kissed Damon on the mouth, before turning to Tate. "Sorry, but Damon's ass is out of bounds. As of now, it's all mine. And if you think we're having a gangbang at the Eagle, think again. I am *not* getting arrested on my wedding night."

Tate pulled a face, and looked to Damon, who shrugged.

"What he said." He waited until Tate had trudged away, before giving me a speculative glance. "My ass is all yours? Where is my boy, and what have you done with him?"

I smiled. "You get your boy in your bed, or the basement, or wherever, anytime you want him. The rest of the time, I'm the man in your life."

Damon's broad smile told me my terms were just fine.

A note about this story

Times are changing. Sex is changing too.
Being HIV positive used to be a death sentence. Not anymore.
We are living in the days of fantastic meds, and u=u. Undetectable means Untransmissible.
Yes, condoms prevent STIs in a way that PrEP doesn't. No one is going to argue that. But frequent testing, knowing your partner–and honest communication–mean going bare is an option for those who want it.

In case you're not familiar with u=u, here's a link
https://www.plushealth.org.uk/undetectable.html

For online support for those living with HIV, their partners, close family friends and carers, there's Plus health.
https://www.plushealth.org.uk/index.html

About the author(s)
(Because now we are three!)

K.C. Wells, writing as Tantalus.

For those who like their stories intensely erotic, featuring hot men and even hotter sex…
Who don't mind breaking the odd taboo now and again…
Who want to read something that adds a little heat to their fantasies…
…there's Tantalus.
Because we all need a little tantalizing.

AMAZON PAGE:
https://www.amazon.com/Tantalus/e/B01IN33IZO
FACEBOOK: **https://www.facebook.com/Tantalus-1603064599937503/**

K.C. Wells started writing in 2012, although the idea of writing a novel had been in her head since she was a child. But after reading that first gay romance in 2009, she was hooked.
She now writes full time, and the line of men in her head, clamouring to tell their story, is getting longer and longer. If the frequent visits by plot bunnies are anything to go by, that's not about to change anytime soon.

If you want to follow her exploits, you can sign up for her monthly newsletter:
http://eepurl.com/cNKHlT

You can stalk – er, find – her in the following places:

Facebook:
https://www.facebook.com/KCWellsWorld

https://www.facebook.com/kcwells.WildWickedWonderful/
Goodreads:
https://www.goodreads.com/author/show/6576876.K_C_Wells
Amazon:
https://www.amazon.com/default/e/B00AECQ1LQ
Instagram: **https://www.instagram.com/k.c.wells/**
Twitter: **https://twitter.com/K_C_Wells**
Blog: **http://kcwellsworld.blogspot.co.uk/**
Website: **http://www.kcwellsworld.com/**

Writing MF as Kathryn Greenway

Kathryn Greenway lives on the Isle of Wight, off the southern coast of the UK, in a typical English village where there are few secrets, and everyone knows everyone else.

She writes romance in different genres, and under different pen names, but her goal is always the same - to reach that Happily Ever After.

Pulled by a Dream is Kathryn's debut novel, although in a whole other life, she is K.C. Wells, a bestselling author of gay romance.

Website: **https://www.kathryngreenway.com/**
Facebook: **https://www.facebook.com/KathrynGreen...**
Twitter: **https://twitter.com/KGreenwayauthor**
Instagram: **https://www.instagram.com/kgreenwayau...**
Goodreads: **https://www.goodreads.com/author/show/17633635.Kathryn_Greenway**
Amazon: **https://www.amazon.com/-/e/B0795VY3TM**

Coming next from Tantalus

Learning the Notes

Steven Torland is about to reach his fiftieth birthday, and to celebrate the occasion, his publicist decides it's time someone wrote a biography of the famous composer and musician. When writer Kyle Mann is approached with the idea, he's flattered and leaps at the chance. It will be his first biography. The idea of spending six months getting to know Steven and researching his history excites him, but there is the added frisson that Steven is sexy as hell. Kyle has always had a thing for older men, and it's no secret that Steven is gay. In his heart Kyle knows it's just a fantasy, but he can still dream, right?

It doesn't take Steven long to realize he wants Kyle in his bed, and Steven usually gets what he wants. But Kyle proves to be more than a convenient fuck. There's something about him that leads Steven to think maybe it's time to let Kyle see the real Steven Torland, the one who is no stranger to the leather community of San Francisco. Steven aims to take things nice and slow, because he doesn't want this one to get away. He wants it all – a lover in his life and a boy in his bed – and he wants to see just how far he can push Kyle, and what Kyle is prepared to do to please him.

Kyle has no idea how much his life is about to change....

Titles by K.C. Wells

From Dreamspinner Press
<u>Learning to Love</u>
Michael & Sean
Evan & Daniel
Josh & Chris
Final Exam

Love Lessons Learned
A Bond of Three
Le lien des Trois
A Bond of Truth
First
Prime Volte
Debt
Dette
Il Debito
Schuld
Waiting for You
The Senator's Secret
Le Secret du Sénateur
Der Verlobte des Senators
Step by Step
Pas à Pas
Schritt für Schritt
Un passo alla volta
Out of the Shadows
Bromantically Yours
BFF
Truth Will Out
My Fair Brady

<u>Collars & Cuffs</u>
An Unlocked Heart
Trusting Thomas
Someone to Keep Me
(K.C. Wells & Parker Williams)
A Dance with Domination
Damian's Discipline
(K.C. Wells & Parker Williams)
Make Me Soar
Dom of Ages
(K.C. Wells & Parker Williams)
Endings and Beginnings
(K.C. Wells & Parker Williams)

Un Coeur Déverrouillé
Croire en Thomas
Te Protéger

<u>Secrets</u> – with Parker Williams
Before You Break
An Unlocked Mind
Threepeat

Avant que tu te brises

Self-published
<u>Personal</u>
Making it Personal
Personal Changes
More than Personal
Personal Secrets
Strictly Personal
Personal Challenges

Une Affaire Personnelle
Changements Personnels
Plus Personnel
Secrets Personnels
Strictement Personnel

Una Questione Personale
Cambiamenti Personali
Piú che personale
Segreti Personali
Strettamente personale
Sfide personali

Es wird persönlich
Persönliche Veränderungen
Mehr als Persönliche
Persönliche Geheimnisse
Streng Persönlich
Persönliche Herausforderungen

Confetti, Cake & Confessions
Confetti, Coriandoli e Confessioni

Connections
Connexion

Saving Jason
Jasons Befreiung
A Christmas Promise
Una promessa di Natale
The Law of Miracles
Truth & Betrayal

Island Tales

Waiting for a Prince
September's Tide
Submitting to the Darkness

Le Maree di Settembre
In Attesa di un Principe
Piegarsi alle tenebre

Lightning Tales
Teach Me
Trust Me
See me
Love Me

Lehre Mich
Vertrau Mir
Sieh Mich
Liebe Mich

Il Professore
Fidati di me

A Material World
Lace
Satin
Silk
Denim

Pizzo
Satin

Spitze
Satin
Seide
Seta

Double or Nothing
Back from the Edge
Switching it up

<u>Anthologies</u>

<u>Fifty Gays of Shade</u>
Winning Will's Heart

Printed in Poland
by Amazon Fulfillment
Poland Sp. z o.o., Wrocław